GHOSTS of WAR

Lost at Khe Sanh

GHOSTS of WAR
Lost at Khe Sanh

STEVE WATKINS

SCHOLASTIC INC.

ISBN 978-0-545-66587-2

12 11 10 9 8 7 6 5 4 3 2 1   15 16 17 18 19 20/0

Printed in the U.S.A.   40
First printing, April 2015
Book design by Yaffa Jaskoll

For my friends Ray Davis and Geoff Seng,
and for so many others who also
served and sacrificed in Vietnam

CHAPTER 1

Band practice wasn't going

well — again. Two weeks after we totally stunk at the All-Ages Open Mic Night, Julie Kobayashi was still trying to convince our friend Greg Troutman that he couldn't sing, and that he *definitely* shouldn't be the front man, or front boy, for our band the Ghosts of War. She was right, of course. Once your voice starts to crack — which was exactly what happened to Greg right in the middle of our first-ever public performance — you need to step away from the microphone already and let somebody else have a turn.

The only problem — besides Greg's cracking voice — was that Julie also kept trying to convince us we should let her be the one on the mic. Unfortunately, Julie can't sing, either. Even more unfortunately, she has what my mom calls a tin ear and can't hear herself when she's singing off-key. What's even *more* unfortunate is she actually thinks she's a great singer. Probably since she's a musical genius in every other way, her parents never had the heart to tell her the truth — that her singing is awful times ten.

Halfway through our third song that day, with Greg still on vocals, Julie suddenly stopped playing, turned off her keyboard, and threw her hands up.

"That sounded like squeaking, not singing," she said, before turning to me and adding, "You tell him, Anderson. He won't listen to me."

I set my guitar down and retreated to the back of our practice room in the basement of my uncle Dex's junk shop, the Kitchen Sink. No way did I want to get in the middle of those two.

Greg bent his guitar pick in half and then tried to bend it straight again. It wouldn't go. "That's just how I sing," he snapped at Julie. "It's my *style*."

"No, it's not," she snapped back. "It's your hormones."

I retreated even farther as they argued back and forth about Greg's "style," until I bumped into something. It was a footlocker. I looked down at it, confused. Just the week before I had moved it to a storage room next door to where we practiced, to get it out of the way and so I wouldn't have to see it all the time and be reminded of what was in there. I had no idea how it got back here. Maybe Uncle Dex had moved it . . .

A few weeks earlier, I'd found a World War II navy pea-coat in the locker, along with a mysterious letter, setting in motion a pretty crazy adventure involving a guy named William Foxwell — or rather the ghost of William Foxwell. Greg, Julie, and I had to solve the mystery of how he went missing in action at the Battle of Midway, which was the most important navy battle of World War II.

I wrote all about it in a notebook that I keep hidden under my mattress at home. I even gave it a title — "The Secret of Midway" — though I doubt I'll ever let anybody read it besides Julie and Greg.

Anyway, I knew there was a lot of other stuff in the locker that looked like it was from other wars, but so far I'd only glanced inside. Greg kept asking me if we could check out what was in there, but I didn't want to go messing around with anything else that might have a ghost attached to it. I was still recovering from the Secret of Midway, and missing

William Foxwell, who sort of became our friend but disappeared once we solved the mystery.

It was funny about that locker, though: The more I stayed away from it, the more I couldn't stop thinking about it, like it had some kind of gravitational pull on my brain — even after I shoved it in that storage room next door. And now here it was, somehow back in the practice room.

Not only that, but as I stood there staring at it, the footlocker started to sort of glow. Then the latch fell open all on its own. Then, the next thing I knew, I was bending down without even thinking about it, opening the lid, and looking inside.

Greg and Julie were still arguing about who squeaked and who squawked when they sang, and so that's what was happening when I found the hand grenade.

I didn't know what it was at first because it was round and smooth, not like the pineapple-looking hand grenades you see in movies. More like a big olive-green lemon. Then I noticed the plunger and safety clip.

There was something written on it, too, scratched into the metal, and I had to take it closer to the front of the practice room to read what it said.

That put a quick end to Julie and Greg squabbling.

"Whoa!" Greg said. "Where did you get that?"

"You shouldn't have that," Julie said before I could answer. "It could be dangerous."

I held the hand grenade up toward the light so Greg and I could read what was on there.

The writing on the grenade said *Z & Fish* and underneath somebody had also written, or scratched, *DMZ 68*.

Greg took off his beanie, which he wore all the time because he said they made us look cool. Or at least less uncool. "What is that supposed to mean?" he asked.

"Beats me," I said. "Maybe we should take it upstairs and ask Uncle Dex."

Julie stomped her foot. "Maybe we should take ourselves upstairs and get away from that bomb before something happens," she said. She was already heading for the stairs.

"It's not a bomb, Julie," Greg said. "It's a hand grenade."

She stopped. "And what is a hand grenade, exactly?"

"Well," said Greg, pulling his beanie back on over his wild red hair, "it's, um, well, I guess it's a bomb. But you throw it. You don't shoot it out of a cannon or whatever."

"Come on," I said. "Let's all go upstairs."

"Leave it down here," Julie said again. "It could blow up and kill us. We have to get out of here."

I couldn't leave the grenade, though. It felt like my fingers were glued to it or something.

And then, as if somebody was standing right behind me, reading over my shoulder, I heard a whispery voice.

"That looks like my lucky grenade."

I whirled around and collided with Greg. Nobody else was there.

"Did you hear that just now?" I asked him.

"Heck, yeah!" he said.

We both looked around for a second, then bolted up the stairs behind Julie.

I still had the grenade.

Uncle Dex saw it as soon as we came up from the basement. He was typing on the computer behind the counter at the Kitchen Sink. He looked up when he heard us, and froze.

In a very calm voice, he said, "Anderson, stop."

So I stopped. I was holding the grenade out in front of me like I wanted to give it to him. He wasn't about to take it, though.

"Okay," he said, still with the calm voice. "Now I want you to very, very slowly and very, very carefully bend down and gently lay the grenade on the floor right where you're standing. Do not take another step. Do not even breathe. Just bend your knees and softly put it down right there."

Julie and Greg inched away from me, and kept inching, all the way to the door. I did what Uncle Dex said: held my breath until I nearly passed out while crouching down to the floor so that I finally could let the hand grenade settle onto the carpet like a big green egg.

"Good," Uncle Dex said. "Very good. Now I want you to tiptoe away from the grenade toward the front door, and while you're doing that I'm going to dial 911."

.   .   .

Uncle Dex was still talking to the police on his cell phone when he joined us outside on the sidewalk.

"Keep moving," he said, pointing across the street. "Over there."

The police showed up two minutes later and they ordered us to move even farther away, a whole block, in fact, as they raced around putting up police tape and stopping cars from driving in front of the Kitchen Sink. There were sirens, more cop cars, ambulances, fire trucks, even the K-9 unit. I couldn't believe it.

Greg just kept saying, "Wow!"

Julie just kept saying, "We are in *so much trouble*!"

I just kept saying nothing at all, knowing Julie was right.

A big crowd of people gathered around us. I tried to slip away at one point, but Uncle Dex grabbed my arm. "Oh, no you don't," he said. "You're staying right here until we get this thing straightened out."

A big black van lumbered up, past all the police cars and fire trucks and everything. An officer moved some police tape to let the van through until it parked right in front of Uncle Dex's store.

Guys dressed like heavily padded ninjas got out, along with a little robot on wheels with cameras and mechanical arms. One of the bomb squad ninjas, operating a remote control, sent the little robot into the Kitchen Sink, or tried to. It kept bumping against the front door until the guy with the remote stepped away from what looked like a monitor next to the van and went over and opened the door for the robot.

The robot disappeared inside.

"What do you think they're going to do?" Greg asked us.

Uncle Dex was now busy talking to a police officer. They kept glancing back over at us — and, I was certain, at me in particular.

"Surveillance," Julie said. Even as nervous as I was, it still bugged me what a know-it-all she could be.

"How do you know?" I asked.

"Isn't it obvious?" she said. "Mounted cameras? Hello?"

I kicked at a loose chunk of sidewalk. "What do they need that for? It's just lying there in the middle of the room, right where I left it."

"Duh," Julie said. "If you *have* expensive police bomb equipment, you have to *use* your expensive police bomb equipment."

"Makes sense to me," Greg said.

We were all three staring intensely down the street to see what was going to happen next when somebody came up behind us. "What did you little worms do now?" a familiar voice asked.

It was Belman, our archenemy, this eighth-grader at our school who had been making fun of us since school started. And what was even worse, he had a band, too, and they were really good. Like *really* good. They won the first battle of the bands at the All-Ages Open Mic Night two weeks ago.

"Hello, Belman," Julie said in this icy voice that almost scared me as much as the whispery ghost voice from earlier. And she wasn't even talking to me!

"Hello, girl worm," Belman said. "Somebody told me you three losers set off a smoke bomb inside that store over there."

"Well, you heard wrong," Greg said. "It was just a hand grenade, and it didn't even explode. So what do you have to say about that?"

Belman just laughed. He had a couple of friends with him who I recognized from his band, the Bass Rats. All their parents were in the military or something and they all used to live on military bases. That's what somebody told us, anyway, and that's supposed to be where they got the name for their band.

"What do I have to say about that?" Belman asked after he and his friends finished laughing. "I say too bad."

"Too bad what?" Julie asked, her voice still icy.

"Too bad it didn't explode," Belman said. "And save everybody from having to listen to your band again."

I was racking my brain to come up with something clever to say, but people around us started pointing and talking so I turned around to look. Julie and Greg and Belman and his friends did, too.

The ninja operating the remote control was opening the door again to Uncle Dex's shop so the robot could roll out onto the sidewalk. Everybody cheered, which seemed kind of dumb since nothing had actually happened as far as I could tell.

The bomb squad got busy attaching a thick metal box to the robot, and back in it went.

Uncle Dex came over to join us. I'm not sure if he'd overheard anything, but I thought maybe he gave Belman a dirty look.

Belman didn't say anything else. He and his friends retreated, then disappeared into the crowd.

"The police are going to need to talk to you three once this is all over," Uncle Dex said. "They're not too happy with me, either."

"How come?" I asked.

He shook his head. "My store, my hand grenade. You guys were just the kids who found it."

"Any idea what they're doing now?" Greg asked. "With that box they brought in?"

"They're going to blow up the hand grenade," Uncle Dex said. "They have some kind of explosive in the bomb box, and they'll detonate that with the remote control after they have the little robot dude pick up the grenade and lock it inside."

I almost said something — that maybe they shouldn't — because that whispery voice from the practice room seemed to be sort of echoing in my head: "That looks like my lucky grenade."

Greg might have been thinking the same thing, because I caught him staring at me, his eyebrows drawn up so his face was one big question mark.

I shrugged and shook my head because what could we do and what could we say?

The ground shook just a little, followed by a dull *TUNK* sound from inside Uncle Dex's store, and that seemed to be the end of it, except for the crashing noise of things falling off the walls at the Kitchen Sink.

"Darn it," Uncle Dex said. "That sounded like my clock collection."

"Okay, folks!" a police officer shouted at the crowds at each end of the street. "Show's over. Time to clear out."

Greg and Julie and I started to leave, even though Uncle Dex had told us earlier that we had to stay. This time it was the police officer giving the command.

"Not so fast, you three. You don't get to leave until we have a little talk. And we'll be calling all your parents about what happened here."

"Oh man," Greg whimpered. "My dad's going to kill me."

Julie patted him on the shoulder. "I'm sure he'll understand after you explain."

"Explain what?" Greg asked.

"That it was Anderson who found the hand grenade," she said. "And who was foolish enough to pick it up."

Greg seemed happy for a second, but then his face fell. "You want me to throw Anderson under the bus?" he said. "That's terrible. I can't do that. I mean, he's my best friend and all."

"But it's the truth," Julie said, as if I wasn't standing right there and could hear the whole conversation.

"Boy, Julie," Greg said. "I don't mean to hurt your feelings by saying this, but sometimes there's *a lot* you don't know about being friends."

CHAPTER 3

Uncle Dex got a warning from the police, and we got a warning from Uncle Dex: "Don't touch anything that might explode, or fire bullets, or stab anybody. I know it's not your fault that the grenade was there in the first place — I didn't know it was there, either — but you have to be smarter about these things. And if something like this ever happens again, you're out of here. No more basement, no more band practice. Got it?"

I'd never seen him mad before, and I wasn't entirely sure he was mad when he said all that now. The police were still there and he had to say something, and sound stern with us and stuff. So maybe it was kind of an act. Or maybe it was half and half.

Either way, we left as soon as they would let us. Julie hadn't said anything since Greg got on her about not knowing how to be a friend, and she barely said good-bye when she climbed on her bike and headed home.

"You think she's mad at me?" Greg asked.

"Probably," I said. "But, hey — she had to hear it. I mean, you have to stick by your friends, right?"

"Right," Greg said. "I guess so."

"Right," I repeated. "So, um, I mean, since you're my friend and all — my *best* friend — I was just wondering . . ."

"Wondering what?" he said, getting suspicious.

"Well, I'm pretty sure we've got another ghost on our hands. You heard the voice back there in the basement. About the lucky grenade. And you have to figure there's a chance that he might show up in my bedroom tonight. You know, like William Foxwell did that first time, asking for me to help him."

"I wasn't there for that," Greg said quickly.

"Yeah, but I told you about it," I said. "And you met him the next day. So anyway, I was hoping you would come over and spend the night so I won't have to be there by myself if this new ghost shows up."

Greg shuddered. "But what if this one isn't friendly like William Foxwell was? What if this one has more hand grenades, and what if he doesn't want us to help him? What if he wants to kill us because we let them destroy his lucky grenade?"

"That's crazy," I said, though Greg made such a convincing case that I wasn't so sure.

"Is it?" he asked. *"Is it?"*

I wasn't about to let him off the hook, though. "Well, that's all the more reason for you to come over," I said. "Don't you think? You wouldn't want me to have to deal with a ghost by myself. Plus, my mom and dad will be home. If anything bad happens, we can call them. They're just down the hall. And Mom's a light sleeper. So will you do it?"

Greg got on his bike. "I guess. I mean yeah, sure. Gotta go home first, though, and let Dad tell me how irresponsible I am. He might even put me on restrictions once the police call him and tell him what happened. It depends on what mood he's in."

"You could still sneak out your window," I said. "Just promise me you'll come, okay?" I wished he'd come with me now, in case the new ghost was already waiting in my bedroom.

Greg let out a giant sigh. "Yes," he said. "I promise. But you owe me."

"Owe you what?" I asked.

"You have to be the one to tell Julie that she can't hold a tune," he said. "And even if my voice is cracking or whatever, her voice is a whole lot worse."

And with that Greg pedaled off into the growing darkness. I climbed on my own bike, but I sure wasn't in any hurry to get home.

·　·　·

Mom and Dad were already sitting down to dinner when I came in. I took off my beanie and slid into my chair at the table, trying to be cool about it, as if I'd been in my bedroom all afternoon doing homework.

Mom put down her fork and knife. "Anderson," she said. "Is there something you want to say to me and your father?"

"Sorry I'm late for dinner?" I said.

Apparently, that wasn't it.

"The police called a few minutes ago," Dad said. "Something about a hand grenade."

I didn't say anything this time.

"You could have been hurt," Mom said, her voice rising. "You could all have been killed. What on earth were you thinking, Anderson?"

"I guess I wasn't thinking," I said, adding a few *I'm sorry*s afterward. I wished I could explain that it almost didn't seem like it was me picking up the grenade, and that it felt glued to my hand — I couldn't have put it down if I'd tried — until we got upstairs and found Uncle Dex. But no way would they understand all that. Or the voice Greg and I heard.

I didn't understand it myself.

Dad lectured me for a while about using my head, and about safety first, and then Mom took over, though she had a hard time getting too steamed up because of her multiple sclerosis. It's this disease she's had for as long as I can remember that affects her muscles and all, and gets pretty bad sometimes so it's hard for her to even get out of bed. I could tell she was fatigued just sitting there setting me straight.

I didn't mind, in a way, because the longer we sat there at the table — and I hadn't even started eating yet — the longer it would be before I had to go to my bedroom and maybe meet another ghost. Thanks to Greg, I was spooked about this new one with (or now without, I guess) his lucky hand grenade, because what if Greg was right and the ghost was mad at us, not friendly at all?

I somehow made it through the rest of the lectures, and dinner, and I even got dessert, though usually when I mess up that's the first privilege to go. Probably Mom and Dad were happy and relieved, deep down, that I was okay and I suppose they were right about what they said before — that we all could have been killed.

"How about if I do the dishes tonight?" I asked once we finished up.

Dad smiled. Usually he and I took turns the nights we were all home to eat together, and Mom wasn't in bed with her MS. Tonight was supposed to be his night.

"I think that's a good idea," he said. "A little penance can do the heart good."

"What's 'penance'?" I asked, already stacking the plates to bring them to the kitchen.

"Doing something good to make up for doing something you shouldn't have done," Dad said, which was kind of what I figured.

I not only cleared the table and rinsed all the dishes and put away all the leftovers, I also unloaded the dishwasher, dried everything and put it away, and reloaded it after that. I even scrubbed the dirty pots and pans. It was a lot of penance, but I wanted to make sure I'd done enough good so the whole hand grenade situation wouldn't come back to haunt me.

CHAPTER 4

Finally, I couldn't put it off any longer, so I went to my room. I hesitated at the door, my sweaty hand on the knob but afraid to open it.

"Please, not another ghost," I muttered to myself. It wasn't a prayer exactly, but it wasn't too far off from being one.

"Okay," I said. "This is it. I'm going in." I held my breath, turned the knob, closed my eyes, pushed the door open, and forced myself to step inside.

I fumbled for the light switch and turned it on, then counted down: "Three, two, one . . ."

There was nobody there. I checked behind the door, in the closet, even under the bed.

Nothing.

But I wasn't about to relax. I texted Greg. *The coast is clear. No ghost so far. Come over soon.*

He texted me back right away. *Did you tell Julie yet that she can't hold a tune?*

I lied and said yes. Then I asked how it went with his dad. Greg said his dad just yelled at him some, but that was all — no restrictions and no punishment except he had to do a few extra chores. Greg said to give him an hour and he'd come over.

•　　•　　•

I was too nervous to do my homework, so I just lay on my bed for a while, still waiting for this new ghost to show up — certain that he would. I kept thinking about his whispery voice from the Kitchen Sink basement: "That looks like my lucky grenade." You can't ignore something like that, or pretend you didn't hear it, no matter how hard you try. Especially after you've already had one ghost show up in your room and hang around for a couple of weeks until you solved his mystery and he could go to his final rest.

I still had the feel of the grenade in my hand, too, and remembered the writing on it: *Z & Fish. DMZ 68.*

What in the world was that supposed to mean?

I couldn't make sense of it, so got up and turned my computer on to do an Internet search. Nothing came up when I typed in "Z & Fish" except a bunch of random stuff that didn't make any sense.

"DMZ 68" was a different story. DMZ was a comic book series set in the future where the five boroughs of New York City were at war with one another, and #68 was one of the issues. It sounded kind of cool, but I had no idea if it was what I was looking for. The last ghost I'd met was from World War II, after all, which was real.

It was hard to imagine that the hand grenade might belong to a character from a comic book. Then again, it had been hard to imagine I'd ever meet up with a ghost in the first place, so anything was possible.

A tapping on my bedroom window jolted me out of all that speculation. I jumped, but it was just Greg. I opened the window and helped him climb in.

"Well?" he asked, looking around.

"No ghost," I said. "Yet."

"Okay," he said, throwing his book bag on the floor and throwing himself on my bed. "So what about Julie? How did she take it when you told her her voice sounds like finger-nails on a chalkboard?"

"Uh, oh yeah, that," I said. "Actually, I kind of might have not quite told her. But I will. I promise. I just have to figure out a way to do it so it won't hurt her feelings."

Greg frowned and crossed his arms over his chest. "I should have known," he said. "You're such a chicken."

"*I'm* a chicken?" I said, incredulous. "I'm sitting here all by myself, waiting for a ghost to show up, and you're calling me a chicken? Thanks a lot, Greg."

He wasn't about to let me get the upper hand, though. "You're a chicken when it comes to standing up to Julie," he said. "You're a Julie chicken."

"Fine," I said. "Why don't you tell her, then?"

"I already have," Greg answered. "Sort of. I mean, I didn't put it quite that way — about the fingernails on the chalkboard and all — but I did tell her she might not be the best person to be our singer. You heard what she said to me about my singing. And speaking of that, how come you didn't stick up for me when she said all that stuff about my voice cracking and all?"

I was about to say that I didn't want to get in the middle of the two of them and their fight over who should be our lead singer, but somebody interrupted me.

· 25 ·

A gravelly voice that didn't sound too happy with the way our conversation was going.

"Will you two ladies give it a rest already," the voice said.

Greg and I both froze, our eyes fixed on something — or rather somebody: a man sitting cross-legged on the floor, leaning against the wall just past the end of my bed.

"Much better," the man said. "I was starting to get a headache having to listen to all that yammering."

"Sorry," Greg whispered.

"Yeah," I said. "Sorry."

The man had an unlit cigar in his mouth. He took it out and looked at it as if he'd just remembered it was there, then he stuck it back in and sort of chomped down on it so it stuck out to the side and he could still talk.

"Either one of you boys happen to have a match?" he asked.

"Sorry," I said again. "I don't think you're allowed to smoke in the house."

The man let out a hollow laugh, which pretty much got rid of any doubt I might still have about him being a ghost.

I guess Greg wanted to be totally sure, though. "Are you, like, you know, a ghost?" he asked.

The man quit laughing and instead fixed his gaze on Greg and stared so hard that I thought Greg might actually melt. Then the man — or the ghost — checked himself out the way he'd looked at the cigar a minute before. He had on an old army jacket with the sleeves torn off and a stained black T-shirt underneath. Plus, camouflage fatigues and boots caked with red mud. Also long, greasy hair held back with a rolled-up bandanna. And a scary-looking knife half as long as my forearm, in a sheath attached to his belt.

A gray, weathered bush hat sat on his knee where he must have taken it off when he came in, or materialized, or however he happened to show up in my room. There was something written on it that I couldn't quite make out.

He looked like he hadn't shaved — or bathed, or changed clothes — in a long time.

After taking inventory of all this — except for his face, of course, which he couldn't see but we could — he nodded.

"A ghost," he said. "I hadn't been able to put a word to it before, but that sounds about right."

"And you need us to help you?" Greg asked, already starting to sound more excited than scared.

The ghost chewed thoughtfully on his cigar for a minute. He had seemed annoyed with us when he first showed up, but I was hoping that had passed. Unlike Greg, I wasn't quite through being scared. Our first ghost had been really young, a sailor, still a teenager. But this guy was older, and harder, and looked a lot meaner.

He didn't answer Greg's question. Instead, he turned his gaze on me and growled again. "Where's my lucky hand grenade?"

CHAPTER 5

"You don't know what happened to the grenade — your lucky grenade?" I asked. "I mean, you were there and everything, right?"

The ghost just looked at me. "You mean when you picked it up out of that footlocker? Yeah, I was there. Sort of."

"But you didn't see what happened when the bomb squad came? After we went upstairs?" I was definitely getting nervous about this.

The ghost kept chewing on that cigar, though it didn't seem to be getting any shorter or anything. "Bomb squad, huh?" he growled. "Don't like the sounds of that one bit.

But, no. Things kind of faded out on me after you boys and that Asian girl ran upstairs."

Julie is actually half Asian — or rather half Japanese since her dad is from Japan and her mom is American. She looks more like her dad than she does her mom.

"I'm sorry," I said to the ghost. "But they, um, I guess you'd say, well, sort of blew it up."

I braced myself for the ghost to yell at me or worse. I had no idea what a ghost might be capable of doing when he got mad at you.

Instead, he waved his hand as if brushing away a mosquito — or dismissing the whole business about the grenade, which is certainly what I hoped.

"I guess it wasn't all that lucky," he said, "come to think of it. Only lucky thing about it was it didn't detonate when I pulled the pin. Don't know why your bomb squad bothered. If it didn't explode back then, I doubt it was going to explode on anybody now."

Greg had sat up on the bed and was leaning in so he could follow every word. "They said it was standard procedure," he said, though I had no idea when he'd heard that from the bomb squad, since we were way down the street when they showed up at Uncle Dex's store. "It's just what they're required to do with unexploded ordnance."

The ghost nodded. "Makes sense," he said. "Can't risk civilians getting hurt."

"So," I started. "About that first time. You said you tried to detonate the hand grenade once before. When was that? And why? And also, who or what is 'DMZ sixty-eight'? And 'Z and Fish'?"

"Whoa!" the ghost said, waving both hands now in front of him. "Slow down there, son! Too many questions. Don't think I can operate that fast anymore."

Greg actually laughed. "He's like that in school, too," he said.

The ghost's face cracked into a smile — literally. Smile lines broke up patches of dried mud on his cheeks. He even managed to look sort of friendly for a second.

But then he chomped back down on his unlit cigar. And he frowned.

"All those questions you just asked me," he said, shaking his head. "I should know all the answers. I know I should, and I almost do — like they're on the tip of my tongue. But I just can't seem to make them all come back to me just yet.

Only how can that be? How can I know that was my lucky grenade, and that I pulled the pin on it one time, and that it didn't explode, but I can't remember anything else?"

"Maybe you just need time to think about it some more," I suggested, trying to be helpful.

"You mean mull it all over?" the ghost asked. "Like I've been mulling it all over for the past, well, guess I can't even say how long."

"How about 'DMZ'? Greg asked. "Could those be your initials, maybe?"

The ghost frowned deeply again. Then he shook his head. "No. Don't think so. In fact, I'm pretty sure they're not."

He brightened a little. "But, hey, it's something to go on, anyway. More than I had this afternoon. And those other things. The 'Z' and the 'Fish.' There's something there, too. Just need to keep digging in my brain until I find it."

He looked at us for a minute. "Guess you boys are ready for bed. Probably got school in the morning, so I'm gonna check out here for a while."

"And mull things over," Greg reminded him, as if he needed reminding.

"Sure," the ghost said, smiling. "And mull things over."

• • •

Greg and I lay in bed for ten minutes with the lights out after the ghost left, neither of us talking, waiting to see if maybe he would come back. He never did — at least not that night.

Actually, Greg was on the floor in my sleeping bag, which was his usual place whenever he stayed over at my house. He only lived a couple of blocks away and kind of had permission to come over whenever his dad was drinking and went into a sort of dark place (that's what Greg called it), which happened once every couple of months. I always offered to get the blow-up air mattress, but he always just said no, he didn't want to be a bother. Even though we were best friends, I knew he was still embarrassed about his dad. This was different, of course — he'd come over because of the ghost — but I guess he was just in the habit of sleeping on the floor by now.

I finally broke the silence. "That ghost didn't sound like he came out of a comic book," I said.

"What are you talking about?" Greg asked.

"It was what I found when I looked it up on the Internet — that 'DMZ 68' that was written on the lucky hand grenade," I explained. "It's a comic book about all the boroughs of New York City being at war with one another."

"That sounds pretty cool, but yeah, probably not that," Greg said. "DMZ must stand for something else. And anyway, that guy — the ghost — he was from a real war."

"But which one?" I said.

"Pretty sure I know," said Greg. "I've seen a lot of pictures of guys that looked kind of like that, not exactly in their regulation uniforms and all."

"Where?" I asked.

Greg didn't answer right away, and I looked over the side of the bed at him. He was staring up at the ceiling.

"Greg?" I said. "Are you okay?"

He nodded. "My dad has all these photographs," he said. "They're in a box he keeps buried in his closet. He probably doesn't know I looked through it. He has a bunch of medals, too. From when he was in Vietnam."

Greg didn't talk about his dad a lot, so I didn't say anything. Just waited for him to finish.

"That ghost," he said. "He was dressed like a lot of the guys in my dad's pictures. I was just thinking he might have served in Vietnam, too."

CHAPTER 6

Greg and I were dragging all
the next day at school. We had lunch with Julie and filled
her in about the ghost, but both of us kept yawning so much
that she finally got annoyed and left our table. "You should
get more sleep," she said, though not in a mean way.

Greg pushed his lunch tray to the side and laid his head
on the table. "Not a bad idea," he said.

It was probably a good thing Julie left when she did
because Belman and a couple of the guys in his band made a
big point of stopping at our table right after.

"Hey, hey, hey," he said, laughing. "It's the Bomb Squad!"

"Go away, Belman," Greg said, not even bothering to open his eyes.

Belman was in eighth grade and we were just lowly sixth graders, so you'd think Greg would be more careful, but that was just how he was, not afraid of anybody. The first time Belman made fun of Greg — actually, made fun of his dad — Greg dumped his food tray all over Belman's shirt.

Belman grabbed the salt shaker and shook salt out on Greg's head. "Show some respect for your elders," he said as his friends burst out laughing. So did some kids at some other tables nearby.

Greg still didn't bother to move or even open his eyes, though he must have known Belman had just done something to him. Or maybe he was too tired to care.

I didn't say anything, hoping the eighth graders would all just go away, which they finally did.

I thought so, anyway. But as soon as I let my guard down, Belman sneaked back up behind me and yelled, "BOOM!"

I nearly wet my pants and Greg fell out of his chair.

Everybody in the whole entire lunchroom laughed this time, Belman and his stupid friends the loudest of all.

• • •

Julie was already at Uncle Dex's store when we finally made it there that afternoon for practice. Greg and I both did a double take because the ghost was standing there in our basement practice room with her.

"Easy, boys," the ghost said. "Don't go passing out on me now."

"Yes, boys," Julie said, sounding almost just like him. "Don't faint or anything. It's just us."

"Just who?" Greg asked once he got his voice back after being startled like that.

"Just me and him," Julie said. "And thanks for nothing, by the way."

"What are you talking about?" I asked. "What did we do?"

Julie sniffed. "Nothing. Just like I said. You could have at least had the decency to say something to my face instead of sending your, your, your —"

She was clearly struggling for the right word. The ghost leaned in expectantly, too.

"Your friend," she said, gesturing toward the ghost.

"Sent him for what — to say what?" I asked.

The ghost took his cigar out of his mouth, examined it, then chomped on it again. "I just explained to your friend here that there are concerns that you boys have about her singing ability."

"Julie," Julie said.

"Julie," the ghost said. "About Julie's singing ability."

Greg took a step back. "Uh-oh."

"Oh, don't be scared, Greg," Julie snapped. "It's all right. I can handle the truth. I'm not a baby or anything."

Greg halted his retreat. "So he told you how awful your voice is and that you shouldn't be our lead singer?"

"Yeah," I chimed in. "And he told you how your voice sounds like fingernails on a chalkboard and everything?"

"And how your parents were probably just being nice to you when they said you had a beautiful voice," Greg said.

"ENOUGH!" Julie shouted. "I get the picture!"

I realized how that must have just sounded — what we said about her singing. And I felt bad that the ghost had been the one to tell Julie in the first place.

"We're sorry, Julie," I said. "I hope that didn't hurt your feelings and all. It's just that, um, well . . ."

Greg finished for me. "It's just that we didn't quite know how to tell you ourselves. Not that we asked the, uh, the ghost to do it for us. Really, Anderson was supposed to be the one to tell you. Only in a nice way."

I thought Julie was going to cry for a second, and I felt even worse for what we'd said. She bit her lip. "It's okay," she said, in a way that I knew it probably wasn't.

Then she said, "It's just that both my dog and my cat got sick last night, so I was already having a hard time today."

Now I felt totally awful. "Oh man, I'm so sorry, Julie. Are they okay?"

"Yeah," said Greg, also sounding worried. "Are they okay?"

Julie shook her head. "No," she said. "They died."

Greg and I were speechless. Greg got his voice back first. "Both of them?"

She nodded.

"The dog *and* the cat?" I asked, kind of stunned.

She nodded again, not looking up. Her hair had fallen around her face.

"We're going to have a funeral service," she said. "I guess you guys can come if you want. I was supposed to sing a hymn, but I probably won't now."

"Oh no," Greg said. "You mean because of what we said about your singing? You shouldn't listen to us. We're total idiots about that kind of thing, Julie."

"Yeah," I said. "Total morons. We don't know anything about anything, especially music and stuff. And really, you should be our lead singer, now that I think about it. You'd be the best. Really. Honest."

"Uh, yeah," Greg said, trying to sound sincere. But what else could he say? Poor Julie lost her dog and her cat in the same night!

Julie was shaking now. I still couldn't see her face because of her hair, but I guessed she was crying.

Then she looked up. She wasn't crying at all. She was laughing!

"You guys really are morons," she said, gasping for a breath. "I don't even have a dog. Or a cat."

Greg and I were speechless again. I wasn't sure I even knew this version of Julie — playing a practical joke on us. A very effective practical joke, judging by how hard the ghost was laughing, and by how red Greg's face was getting, and probably mine, too.

"Not funny, Julie," I said while gritting my teeth.

"Oh, I don't know about that," the ghost said. "Seemed pretty funny to me."

"She definitely got us back," Greg admitted.

I might have growled then. Julie just grinned.

The ghost stepped forward, sort of between us, and did

that exaggerated throat-clearing thing people do when they want to interrupt — which was good, because I wasn't sure what I was going to say next.

"Maybe we could get down to a little business?" he said in that gruff voice of his.

"What's the business?" Greg asked. "I mean, is it something different this time, or the same as the last ghost we had?"

The ghost looked confused until Julie explained. "There was another ghost," she said, already moving on from practical jokes and revenge and stuff. "From World War II. We helped him find out what happened in the war, how he came to be missing in action. And then he was able to find his peace, and finish his journey."

The ghost nodded as he seemed to be chewing not just on his cigar but also on what Julie had said. "That's pretty much the situation," he said at last. "I guess I could use your help. It's been pretty hard, I have to admit, being in this place. In between and all. Neither here or there, you might say."

I finally set down my guitar case. Greg did, too. "Maybe we can start by seeing if you've been able to remember anything else about the grenade," Greg said.

The ghost nodded, with a serious look on his face. He chomped down harder on his cigar, not that I could see a difference when he took it out of his mouth and studied it.

"Actually, something did come to me," he said. "That word, 'Fish.' It kept swimming around in my head, you might say, until finally it hit me."

"What?" I asked.

"That was his name," the ghost said. "What we called him, anyway."

Greg pulled off his beanie and scratched his head, obviously confused. "Him who? Whose name?"

"My buddy," the ghost said. "With the grenade. Well, what I mean is it was *my* grenade, but he was with me when I had the grenade."

"And when was that?" Julie asked.

"Not quite sure," the ghost said. "I remember where, though. Sort of. What the terrain was like, anyway. I remember there were mountains, a lot of mist, real thick jungle, waterfalls, that sort of thing. And I remember they had us surrounded."

"Who had you surrounded?" I asked.

"Was it the North Vietnamese?" Greg chimed in. "I bet that's who it was."

The ghost thought really hard for a minute, then he nodded and said, "Maybe."

Then he continued, "Now mind you, it's kind of like a snapshot I've got going here and not much else. Not right at this minute. But what I remember is just me and him — Fish — hugging the ground, our faces pressed so hard into it we were practically eating dirt, and trying to make ourselves invisible. We could hear them looking for us, what sounded like them jamming their bayonets into all the bushes around us. I didn't dare even breathe and neither did Fish. They kept coming closer and closer. No way they were not going to find us. And if they found us, no telling what they would do, but we knew it wouldn't be good."

I realized I'd been holding my breath from the minute the ghost started his story. My palms were sweating, too.

"That sounds more like a movie than a snapshot," Julie observed.

"Maybe so," said the ghost. "Little piece of a movie, anyway. Scene from a movie, maybe. Anyway, it was dark, but not dark enough. We could see out through those bushes — their pants' legs and boots — that's how close they were. And if we could see them, it was only seconds before they took a long and hard look inside the bushes and saw us, too.

Never mind the bayonets. They would shoot. Only we probably wouldn't be lucky enough to get killed outright. So I felt for it on my vest — my last grenade. Just barely moved my hand. Inching it along. Not wanting to so much as rustle a blade of grass or a leaf or anything.

"Fish saw what I was doing and we locked eyes and without saying anything I asked him if I should do it — go ahead and pull the pin and blow us both up before they got to us, and hopefully blow a bunch of them up, too. And with his eyes he told me back — 'Do it!'

"So I did. I pulled the pin and didn't even hesitate, just let go of the plunger —"

He paused and took a deep breath, almost as if he wanted to make the story more dramatic on purpose.

Greg was practically bouncing up and down on his amplifier. "And then what?" he asked.

"Yes, is there more you remember?" Julie asked in her kindest voice.

The ghost laughed. "Yeah. I remember the grenade didn't blow us all up. Didn't blow up at all. It was a dud."

Greg was the first to speak. "And you got captured? Is that what happened to you and your friend?"

The ghost shook his head. "That's the good part," he said. "We were all ready to die for the cause — whatever the cause might have been, since I can't remember — and instead nothing happened, and we were so stunned we just laid there not believing it, and meanwhile the enemy just sort of moved off into the jungle and we were left there still hugging dirt and pinching ourselves to make sure we were still alive and didn't dream the whole thing up."

"Wow," said Greg.

"Yeah," I agreed. It was a pretty amazing story.

Julie had another question. "What about 'Z'?" she asked. "Do you remember anything about a 'Z'?"

"Oh yeah," the ghost said, as if it was no big deal. "That was me."

CHAPTER 7

We ran through every Z name
we could think of, but none of them worked. The ghost —
Z — didn't recognize any of them, anyway. Zeke, Zebediah,
Zach, Zane.

"How about Zephyr?" Greg suggested.

"Zephyr?" Z repeated, sounding tired. He was starting
to fade.

"What about Zeus?" Greg asked. "Do you think it could
be that?"

Z shook his head. He said something but none of us
could make out what it was.

And then he was gone.

After a few minutes, we got the instruments out and plodded through a half-hour practice — with nobody singing — then decided to knock off early. We all agreed we would look up whatever we could find about Vietnam, and then compare notes the next day. Z still couldn't say for sure if he'd served there — and gone missing from the Vietnam War — but it seemed like the best bet.

"I'll see if my parents will take me to the library after dinner," Julie said.

"And I'll be looking stuff up on the Internet," said Greg.

"You could also ask your father," Julie suggested.

Greg shook his head. "No way. He won't talk about that. Pretty much ever. I brought it up one time when I was little and do you know what he said?"

"What?" Julie asked.

"Nothing," Greg said. "He didn't say a word. He just looked at me for a minute and then walked away. The only way I even knew he had been in Vietnam was because my mom told me."

Greg's parents were divorced. His mom had a new family and lived in Indiana, which was where Greg went for a couple of weeks every summer to visit, but that was about it. The rest of his time he was here in Virginia living with his dad, who was a lot older than most of the parents we knew. Closer to grandparent age, actually.

"It might be good to ask him again," Julie suggested, trying to be helpful.

"Probably not," Greg insisted. What he didn't say, but what I knew he meant, was that he was afraid if he brought up Vietnam with his dad, then it might make his dad start drinking.

"Well, there is one other thing," Julie said, dropping the subject.

"Which is what?" I asked.

"Which is that you have to be the new lead singer, Anderson, since Greg's voice keeps cracking," Julie said, "and since, apparently, the two of you have decided that I am not a good singer, even though I know that I am. Only a different kind of good singer than you are used to."

"Uh, I don't think I can do that," I said about me taking over as the lead singer.

"And why not?" Julie demanded. Greg just looked on, not saying anything.

"Because I have a really high voice for singing," I said. "Like in the kids' choir at church I have to sing the high parts of the hymns."

Greg laughed. "He's a soprano."

Julie didn't laugh, but I did see her crack a small smile. "Good. We will need something to make us stand out, besides the excellent songs that I have written, of course. And your soprano boy voice will be it."

And with that she took off. Greg did, too, still laughing.

"Catch you later, Soprano Boy," he said as he headed up the stairs.

I started to follow him, but I hadn't packed up my guitar yet so I had to stay. Plus, I wanted to see if the ghost might come back now that everybody had left.

He didn't.

. . .

Uncle Dex was busy at his computer behind the counter at the front of the store when I finally went upstairs with my guitar. Nobody else was around. He did a lot of his business selling stuff over the Internet. I used to worry that he didn't have too many walk-in customers and that he might not be able to keep the store open. It had belonged to Pop Pop, Uncle Dex's and my mom's dad and my granddad, who died last year.

Uncle Dex reassured me, though, that he was doing just fine, so I believed him. I would hate for our family to ever lose the Kitchen Sink.

"I didn't hear much practicing down there today," Uncle Dex said.

I set my guitar case down and leaned against the counter. "Yeah. We had to discuss some things."

"Like what?" Uncle Dex asked, not looking up from his computer screen.

"Like who's going to be the singer," I said. "And they decided it was going to be me."

Uncle Dex looked up and smiled. "Congratulations. Was this something you were wanting to do?"

"Not exactly," I said. "Actually, not at all. Julie and Greg are already calling me Soprano Boy. Julie says we need something to help us stand out, and I'm it."

Uncle Dex kept smiling. "Maybe if you guys just play loud enough, nobody will notice the singing and you'll be okay."

I brightened up when he said that. "Great idea," I said. "I'll just turn my amplifier all the way up when I play."

"Just maybe not downstairs while you're practicing," Uncle Dex said. "Wouldn't want to scare the customers."

"Right," I said. And then I changed the subject. "So, do you know much about Vietnam?"

"Whoa," he said. "That was fast. From Soprano Boy to the war in Vietnam in one sentence."

"Yeah," I said. "Well, I was just wondering about it. We haven't exactly studied it in school or anything."

"I don't think they like to talk about it too much these days," Uncle Dex said. "You know, since it's the one war we lost and all."

"We lost?" I asked. "America lost a war?"

"That's what they say." Uncle Dex had stopped doing work and was facing me now. "Twelve long years of fighting, and that was just the years that U.S. troops were there — starting in 1961 until we left in 1973."

He paused and then asked me, "You do know where Vietnam is, don't you?"

I shook my head. "Not exactly."

So Uncle Dex pulled a map of Asia up on his computer. He pointed first at China, which took up most of the space. "You know what this is, of course."

"Of course," I said. "It's North Dakota."

Uncle Dex smiled. "Funny guy," he said.

Then he pointed at a land mass, sort of a very wide peninsula, hanging down below the eastern part of China.

"This is Southeast Asia. On the right side going all the way down is Vietnam — fat at the top, narrow in the middle, fat at the bottom." He pointed to the expanse of blue to the right of Vietnam and said, simply, "South China Sea."

To the left of Vietnam were a couple of other countries whose names I'd heard of before but hadn't ever seen on a map: Laos and Cambodia tucked right up next to Vietnam, and Thailand on the other side of them.

"So who were we fighting?" I asked, feeling dumb for not knowing.

"North Vietnam," he said. "The country was divided into two — North and South. We were fighting to protect South Vietnam from the North taking it over and making the whole country communist."

"Sounds complicated," I said.

Uncle Dex took off his baseball cap and scratched his head. "It was. Because not everybody agreed that the war was all about stopping the spread of communism. Some said it was like the Civil War here in the U.S., and basically none of our business. People felt like we shouldn't send our troops over there and get involved. That it was between North and South Vietnam. And since South Vietnam had its own army, they should fight their own fight. There were a lot of antiwar protests in the U.S., especially in big cities and colleges."

"Why didn't we win the war?" I asked.

"That's complicated, too," Uncle Dex said. "North Vietnam was getting weapons from Russia and China, which both had communist governments, and the U.S. was worried about the spread of communism all over the world. You probably heard about the Cold War. Well, that's what it was — us versus the communists in different countries, seeing who could control the type of government."

I *had* heard about the Cold War in school, so at least I knew a little something.

"Anyway, we bombed the cities in North Vietnam a lot," Uncle Dex continued, "but couldn't invade because if we did, then we'd probably be at war with Russia and China, too, and it would be World War III and nobody wanted that."

My head was already spinning with all this information about the war in Vietnam, but the more Uncle Dex talked, the more questions I had.

"It was mostly what you'd call a guerilla war," he explained. "Out in the jungle and in villages and rice paddies and mountains all over South Vietnam. A lot of time we didn't even see the enemy. Just snipers and land mines and booby traps and assassinations. The Viet Cong — those were North Vietnam's guerilla fighters — didn't wear regular uniforms, and just dressed like peasants. It was almost impossible to know if somebody you met was a friend or an enemy. Except in the North, in this area called the Central Highlands, which sort of connected the two halves of the country. The official North Vietnamese Army was up there, with regular uniforms and all, and there were some actual open battles between us and them."

Uncle Dex was moving his hands to pretend he was drawing an outline of Vietnam, but it was still hard to follow what was supposed to be happening where in Vietnam. "Mostly what we were doing was trying to hit a moving target," he continued. "Trying to control various areas of the country, stomp out guerilla activity. But we'd get control over one area or one province and things would start happening in another area, another province."

"Did *we* wear regular uniforms?" I asked, thinking about the ghost and what he had on — which was like half a uniform and half just whatever. "I mean, our soldiers and all?"

"Mostly," Uncle Dex said. "But things kind of broke down in places, especially out in the jungles when our guys were on patrols for long periods of time, or sometimes even living with local people to try to find out who was our friend and who was our enemy. A lot of those guys would quit wearing regular uniforms and just wear whatever was comfortable or whatever they felt like. And a lot of them even grew their hair long and grew beards and mustaches and stuff, which they kept that way while they were out away from everything, until they were ordered back with the rest of the army or marines or whoever they were with."

"How come?" I asked.

"Some I'm sure did it just because they were out in the jungle, like I said, and didn't have access to things like barbers and razors and anywhere to wash their clothes. Some just didn't like the military or the war because they'd been drafted and didn't want to be there."

"Can I ask you just one more question?" I said.

"Sure," Uncle Dex replied. "As long as it's a quick one. Your mom and dad are going to wonder where you are, and I've got someplace to be so I need to close up the shop."

I thanked him for staying around as long as he had and then asked, "Do you have any idea what 'DMZ 68' might mean? I saw it written somewhere in something about Vietnam, or rather about the war in Vietnam."

"It stands for Demilitarized Zone," Uncle Dex said as he shut down his computer, thankfully not bothering to ask me where I'd seen it. "It was this narrow area, up in the Central Highlands, not even a mile wide, between the borders of North and South Vietnam. There weren't supposed to be any troops in that area, or zone, which was why they called it the DMZ. It was supposed to be neutral there."

"And the '68' part?" I asked.

"Not sure about that," he said, "but the worst of the fighting happened in 1968 and spilled over into 1969. That was when most of the American troops were there — more than half a million of our guys."

"That's a lot," I said, stating the obvious.

And I was certain now that I had met one of them. The ghost of one, anyway.

CHAPTER 8

"Vietnam, huh?"

The ghost was in my bedroom, sitting on the floor again, his back against the wall, that unlit cigar still clenched between his teeth on one side of his mouth.

"We're pretty sure," I said. "I mean, everything fits. The Demilitarized Zone and 1968. Plus, your, well, your sort of uniform."

He glanced down at what he was wearing and plucked at a loose thread on his vest. There were a lot of loose threads at all the holes and tears in it. None came out when he pulled, though.

"That's good detective work," he said. "Vietnam is

coming back to me. Kind of. And when you say DMZ, that has a ring of something familiar. As though maybe that's where we were then?"

He said it as a question. I asked a question back.

"Where you were when what?"

"When my lucky grenade didn't blow us up to smithereens," he said. "Me and Fish."

"Do you remember anything about him yet?" I asked. "Like his real name, maybe?"

Z chomped harder on the cigar, which I'd noticed he often did when he was thinking hard about something, as if it might help. It didn't. He took the cigar out and examined the chewed end, then popped it back in his mouth, which usually meant he was done.

But not this time.

"Something else I remember," he said, "was that time with the lucky grenade — it wasn't the only time me and Fish were out there like that. It's hard to bring it all into focus, but I'm pretty certain there were other guys with us. Sometimes. Not ever a lot. Small team of guys, you might say. Operating at night. And we did some things I kind of don't want to talk about, and I kind of wish I didn't remember."

He paused. "There were some people," he said, speaking really slowly. "Some bad people. In some villages. I guess it was Vietnam, like you said. That sounds about right. Still not coming back to me all the way, but some. But anyway, these bad guys — it was our job to make sure they didn't do any more bad things. It was our job to make them stop. To make them disappear . . . And that's all I'm going to say on that subject."

He had already started into his ghost-fade again.

"Wait," I said. "Can't you hold on a little while longer?"

It was too late, though, and in another second he was gone. I stared at the place where he'd just been, wishing he'd come back. Who knew how much time we might have to find out Z's full name, and Fish's, and what exactly happened to them in Vietnam. The last time, with William Foxwell, we had a couple of weeks, but what if that was the exception? What if usually with these ghosts you only got a couple of days to solve the mystery of who they were and what happened to them?

I lay down on my bed, a wave of exhaustion washing over me. I hadn't gotten much sleep the night before, and it was pretty late already tonight. I thought about texting Greg and Julie, but my head felt too heavy, and then the rest of me did, too. I pulled the covers over me and fell asleep.

I had a dream, or a fragment of a dream, where I was in the jungle that Z described, where he and his buddy Fish were surrounded by the enemy — the Viet Cong or the North Vietnamese Army — and we were hiding in the bushes. It was hot and hard to breath. There was no lucky grenade this time, just the enemy coming closer and closer and closer and closer, and even though I'd only just gotten there, time was already running out —

.　　.　　.

Next thing I knew it was morning and Mom was sitting next to me on my bed.

"Are you all right, Anderson?" Mom was asking me. She seemed to have said it a couple of times already.

"Yeah," I said, struggling to sit up. "What's going on?" I was totally confused and couldn't remember what day it was or figure out what time it was, even though sunlight streamed through the bedroom window. And I couldn't figure out why Mom was up. Because of her MS and how tired it always made her, she could hardly ever get up in the mornings before I left for school.

Mom brushed the hair off my forehead. "You shouted something in your sleep," she said. "I came in to check on you. And it's also time for you to get up and get some breakfast if you're going to catch the school bus."

I remembered now about the dream and wondered if I might have yelled something in the middle of that.

"Thanks, Mom," I said, sliding back down under the covers. "I'm okay. Must have been a bad dream."

"Oh, no you don't, Anderson," Mom said in a voice that was way too cheerful for this early in the morning. "We're having breakfast together for once, so no going back to sleep."

She stood up and pulled the covers off of me. Even the sheet.

"Mom!" I grumbled.

"Don't 'Mom' me," she said. "I've already got waffles in the toaster oven."

Five minutes later, Mom and I were drowning our waffles in syrup. I guess it was kind of a special occasion, her getting up so early to have breakfast with me, because Mom even let me spray whipped cream on top of mine.

"But no sugar crashing in the middle of class," she warned.

I couldn't say anything because my mouth was too full. It was delicious.

When I could finally talk I asked Mom what she remembered about the Vietnam War.

"The things that pop into your head," Mom said. "It's hard to keep up with you sometimes. Is this something you're studying in school?"

"Not exactly," I said, wanting to be as honest as I could. "But it kind of came up. You know."

"Well," Mom said, "I can't say I remember a whole lot. I was really young, probably not even out of preschool when the war ended. I do remember my parents arguing a lot about it even after the war was over, when North Vietnam conquered South Vietnam. Your grandfather had served in the military during the Korean War, but that was before Vietnam. He supported the war, but my mother wasn't so sure we should have been over there. One of her brothers — your great-uncle Dexter — was drafted, and he went over when he was eighteen. She always said he just wasn't the same when he came back. He had always been this really happy guy, but then after Vietnam he got super quiet and stopped coming to family gatherings, even Christmas. It was very sad."

"Did they name Uncle Dex after him?" I asked.

"Yes," Mom said. She had stopped eating and was just pushing bites of her syrupy waffle around on her plate, suddenly quiet. I wished I hadn't brought up the subject of the war.

"What happened to him?" I finally asked, though I was afraid it might make Mom even sadder.

"He passed away when you were very little," she said. "You never knew him, but he did get to see you once, and hold you. He was in the hospital then. He had a hard time breathing. It got worse and worse. They said it was from being exposed to something called Agent Orange when he was in the war."

I stopped eating, too. "Agent Orange?"

"Yes," Mom said. "It was a chemical the Air Force sprayed over a lot of Vietnam to kill off vegetation in areas where our troops were searching for the enemy. It was so the North Vietnamese and the Viet Cong wouldn't be able to hide so well in the forests and jungles. I don't think our government knew, or didn't think about, the effect it would have on the people who ended up breathing it. Like your great-uncle. Respiratory diseases. Cancers. Skin diseases. All sorts of terrible things."

I didn't ask any more questions, but I did give Mom the biggest hug I could when I got up to go catch the bus to school. I used to think going to war must be really exciting, like in Call of Duty. But after meeting these ghosts, and now talking to Mom about her uncle and Agent Orange, I was starting to think maybe I had it all wrong.

CHAPTER 9

That day at lunch, I filled Greg and Julie in on my conversation the night before with the ghost. Greg sat with his back to us at our table next to the cafeteria wall, his chair turned instead so he could keep a lookout on the lunch line and all the other tables — so Belman and his gang wouldn't be able to sneak up on us again and sprinkle salt on our heads or whatever.

"Z and Fish," Julie murmured. She had her lunch roll stuck to the end of her fork and occasionally brought it close enough to her mouth so she could take a small, thoughtful nibble.

"So we know he was in Vietnam in 1968," she said. "And we know he was in the Demilitarized Zone and at some point he and his friend Fish were surrounded by the enemy. In the jungle. And we know they went on what sounds like some sort of secret missions. Like maybe to assassinate people."

"He didn't exactly say that," I corrected her.

"But it did sound like it, right?" Julie asked.

"Yeah," I said. "I guess. He didn't want to go into any details or anything."

"And how old would you say Z is, or was?" Julie asked. "That might be something that could help us."

Greg turned around to look at Julie and me. We all looked at one another. "I'm no good at telling how old grown-ups are," Greg admitted. "I mean, I know my dad is a lot older than Anderson's dad, older than everybody's dad, but I couldn't say that he looks a lot older or anything. He just looks old. They all do."

"Yes," said Julie. "They all just look grown-up."

"Not Uncle Dex," I said.

We all agreed that Dex was the exception.

"But they were mostly young in Vietnam," Julie said. "The average age of soldiers was only nineteen. So this Fish could have been very young."

"Why were they all so young?" I asked.

Greg answered. "Because of the draft. All the guys had to register with the government back then once they turned eighteen, and then they picked birthdays and the ones whose birthdays they picked had to serve in the army for two years, and most of them went to Vietnam for one of those years."

Greg was turned back around, his back to me and Julie, when he said this. "I kind of know a lot about Vietnam," he added. "Because of my dad. Since he wouldn't talk about it I had to read a bunch of stuff on my own. Not that I know everything, of course."

"Well, what else do you know that might be helpful?" I asked.

Greg shrugged. "I was thinking maybe we should take a field trip."

"To where?" Julie asked, still nibbling on her roll.

"To The Wall," Greg said.

That one threw me off. "Why would we go to a wall?" I asked.

Greg laughed. "Not *a* wall. *The* Wall. The Vietnam Veterans Memorial, up in DC. They call it The Wall."

Julie apparently knew about it, too. "It's a long wall of black marble cut into the side of a hill in a forested part of the National Mall, near the Lincoln Memorial," she said. "The names of all the Americans who died in Vietnam are carved into the marble. Great idea, Greg. Many people go there to find the name of their relative or friend who died, and to leave flowers or notes at the base of The Wall. It's supposed to be a very powerful memorial."

"What do you mean 'powerful'?" I asked, hating to be the odd man out in knowing all this stuff.

Julie laid her hand over her heart. "Very emotional," she said. "Because it is so different from most memorials. It doesn't celebrate the war. It remembers those who lost their lives there."

"So you think we should go?" I asked the back of Greg's head. He was still keeping an eye on the cafeteria.

"Yeah," he said. "Maybe your uncle Dex can drive us like he did when we went on that trip with the first ghost. Remember? When the ghost rode with us?"

"He wasn't with us the whole time," I reminded Greg. "He faded in and out."

"Yes," Julie said, "but he was there, and perhaps our new ghost, Z, might recognize some names on The Wall, and it might help loosen some more of his memories, so that we can help him find out what happened."

"When should we go?" I asked.

"Soon," Greg said.

"Yes, right away," said Julie. "We don't know how much time we have, Anderson, and you said yourself that when he visited you last night he faded out very quickly at the end, and for no reason that you could see."

•　　•　　•

Z didn't show up that night in my bedroom. I waited and waited until my yawns started to run together and I was having a hard time keeping my eyes open.

I decided I would talk to him even though he wasn't there, on the chance that maybe he *was* there, just not in a state where I could see or hear him.

"So, we're going to this place up in Washington," I said to the room. "It's this memorial for Vietnam War veterans like you, only it's the ones who were killed, and just so you know, your name might be on there. We're hoping you'll be able to come with us and let us know if it helps you remember anything. My uncle is driving us this weekend, on Saturday."

I waited for a minute to see if Z would show up, or say something, or even if there might be one of those breezes in the room that might or might not be him. That was the way it worked with our other ghost. He could be near us some-times, but not visible and not able to show himself except for a little gust of wind or whatever.

But I got nothing.

"Okay, then," I said. "I'm heading for bed. Please don't wake me up, if you can help it. I'm kind of tired from not really sleeping the past couple of nights, and if I fall asleep in class again, I'm going to probably get in trouble at school. You could go over to Greg's house if you want. He might not mind it if you did, and if you woke him up. I probably wouldn't do that at Julie's, though. I'm not too sure, but I'm guessing she would probably get mad at you for waking her up in the middle of the night."

I waited a few more minutes, and then crawled into bed.

Something thumped against my window and I practi-cally jumped back up again, but it was just a branch banging into the side of the house from outside, and most likely the wind causing it for real.

I sank back down into bed. This ghost business was exhausting.

CHAPTER 10

We were barely on the inter-state two days later, heading fifty miles north with Uncle Dex to Washington, DC, when he asked if we wanted to learn some Vietnam War songs.

"Sure," said Greg, sounding genuinely interested.

"Uh, okay, I guess," I said, trying not to sound embarrassed, though of course I was.

"Thank you, sir," Julie said, sounding very formal and polite. Then she added, "But I have been told that I should not be allowed to sing in public."

Uncle Dex drummed on the steering wheel. "Who

told you that?" he demanded. "Of course you should sing. Everybody should sing, whether they can hold a tune or not."

Julie stiffened in the backseat. "Were you told that I cannot hold a tune?" she asked.

Uncle Dex shook his head. "Wasn't told anything," he said. "Just making a point. My dad — Anderson's Pop Pop — was tone-deaf as could be, but when we went to church he made us sit on one of the pews right up front, and whenever there was a hymn, he would totally belt it out. Embarrassed Anderson's mom, but not me. I sang as loud as I could to try to keep up with him."

He winked back at me in the rearview mirror. "Now who wants to sing?"

The first song was called "The Ballad of the Green Berets," and it was about soldiers in the army wanting to be selected for this elite fighting unit they called the Green Berets that did a lot of stuff during the Vietnam War. Uncle Dex said they were supposed to be these awesome guerilla fighters, and right away I wondered if maybe Z might have been a Green Beret. Those secret missions he went on, under cover of darkness, working with just a few other men. It sure sounded like it.

Unfortunately, he wasn't around for us to ask, or if he *was* in the car I hadn't seen him yet. I just hoped he'd manage to be there somehow.

After that, Uncle Dex taught us an antiwar song that demonstrators used to sing on college campuses and stuff to try to get the president to end the war. It had a really long, funny name — "I-Feel-Like-I'm-Fixin'-to-Die Rag" — and it was making fun of people who wanted to go to war, and generals and people who made bombs and stuff like that.

I got a weird feeling in the middle of that one that was hard to explain, but like maybe Z was there after all, even though I still couldn't see him, and he didn't like the song one little bit.

"Uh, Uncle Dex?" I said, interrupting. "Any chance we could sing something else besides this one?"

Uncle Dex said sure, but the next one was an antiwar song, too, and somebody or something didn't seem to like that one, either, because we suddenly seemed to be hitting every bump and crack and pothole on the highway and it didn't stop until we finished with the last verse.

When we finally got to Washington we miraculously found a parking space on Constitution Avenue, not far from the Vietnam Veterans Memorial.

"This way," Julie said when we got out of the car, even though we could all see the sign and the arrow.

We were practically standing on the memorial before we realized it, because the sidewalk we were on just sort of gradually sloped down into this little valley next to the black granite wall that started off really short and then grew at the lowest — or highest — point to where it was way above our heads. Even with the descriptions from Julie and Greg, I was still expecting a statue or something, but it was just as they'd said — a sort of gash in the side of this hill and all the names of America's Vietnam dead neatly chiseled into it, arranged in order of when they died.

The Wall was polished so clean that as you stood there looking at all the names — nearly sixty thousand of them — you also saw yourself, staring right back at you. It was impossible to not reach out and touch The Wall and trace some of the names with your fingers, which also meant you were sort of touching a part of yourself as well when you did that.

All of us got really quiet. There were a lot of other people there, too, but except for a few people whispering, we couldn't hear anybody or anything besides our own breath and the distant sound of cars on the road.

Uncle Dex spoke to us softly. "There are directories up

the hill," he said, pointing in the direction of the far end of The Wall, toward the Lincoln Memorial. "You can look up a name and find out where that person was from and when exactly he or she died."

"Are there many women on here?" Julie asked.

"Not a lot," Uncle Dex said. "I think just eight or nine. Most of them were nurses helping out the sick and wounded. There's actually a statue up the hill, too, for the women who served in Vietnam. We can go see it whenever you guys want. There's a statue of some soldiers, too, that they added after they built The Wall. But The Wall is still what people come to see."

"And to touch," Greg added.

·   ·   ·

After about fifteen minutes, we walked up the hill to look at the statues Uncle Dex had described, and to get a closer look at the Lincoln Memorial farther on, and this long reflecting pool that runs from the Lincoln Memorial up the Mall, practically to the Washington Monument.

I kept wanting to go back to The Wall, though. I wasn't sure why. It was just this sort of gravity thing pulling me there, or that's how it felt. Greg must have felt it, too, because while Uncle Dex and Julie stayed next to the Vietnam Women's Memorial, Greg and I wandered back down to The Wall.

We stopped for a couple of minutes and waited while what looked like a family stood all together blocking the walk. They were holding one another and taking turns tracing a name on The Wall with their fingers. A girl about our age held a sheet of paper over the name and rubbed over it with a piece of charcoal so the name made an impression when she peeled it off. She showed it to an older lady who might have been her grandmother, and the grandmother hugged her especially hard. They all eventually left, except the grandmother, who knelt down in front of The Wall below the name they had been touching and tracing. I was pretty sure she was praying at first, and then, looking up, whispering something in the direction of the name.

When she got up to go join the rest of her family she left something behind: an old photo. Greg and I saw it when we walked past after they were gone. It was a young man in an army uniform, hugging a woman in a wedding dress. They both looked really, really young.

"Do you think the girl in the wedding dress was her?" Greg asked me, gesturing toward the retreating back of the woman who had left the photo.

"Maybe," I said, looking at the name that had drawn the family there. I pointed. "And I bet that was the guy in the picture."

"I wonder how long they were married?" Greg asked.

"Well, if that was them, then I guess long enough to have a family," I said. "But not long enough to get to raise their kids together and watch them grow up."

An older man in a faded army jacket came up to us. He wore a name tag that read "Jan Scruggs." "Hi, kids. I'm Jan, one of the volunteers," he said. "Is there anything I can help you with today?"

Greg jumped right in with the questions. "What do you do with stuff like that?" he asked, pointing to the photo the woman had left behind.

Jan nodded. "Good question," he said. "Flowers and stuff, we let them be until they wilt, and then we have to remove those. Other things, like pictures and poems, we collect and they go into an archive that the National Park Service set up. None of that gets thrown away."

"What other kinds of things?" Greg asked.

"Oh, you'd be surprised," Jan said. "Pretty much you name it, we've seen it. Lots of pictures. Dog tags. Letters.

Baby shoes. Awards. I have a few buddies on The Wall so I've been volunteering here a long time."

"We're sorry for your loss, sir," Greg said solemnly.

"Thank you," Jan said with a thoughtful nod. "Are there other questions I can answer for you?"

"There are these diamond shapes next to most of the names, and crosses next to some, not nearly as many. Can you tell us what those are for?" I asked.

"Another good question," he said. "The diamonds are next to the names of those that were killed and their deaths could be confirmed. The crosses are the ones who went missing. If any of them ever turned back up somehow, they're supposed to change the cross to a circle to show they're still alive after all."

"How many circles are there?" I asked.

He shook his head. "None."

.   .   .

We thanked the volunteer and he walked on in the direction of the family we had seen earlier, and all at once it seemed as if nobody was there any more, just us.

But then, as if he'd just shown up out of nowhere — which I guess in a way he had — we saw Z, kneeling next to The Wall to the east, about halfway up the hill from the lowest point, tracing a name with his shaky hand. Greg and I looked at each other, rubbed our eyes, and looked back. He was still there, still touching that one particular name. We walked closer, our reflections walking with us in the black granite, but once we got close enough we saw that there was no reflection of Z, which was pretty spooky on the one hand, and pretty much made sense on the other.

"Hey," Greg said softly once we were standing right next to Z.

"Hey, boys," Z said without looking back at us, as if he'd been expecting we'd show up.

I glanced around and noticed a few people at the opposite end of The Wall, but if they thought anything weird was going on — like that we were standing there with a ghost — they didn't do or say anything to show it. I was betting that they couldn't see him. As we stood there Z had already started flickering in and out of view.

"I know this one," Z said, indicated the name he had been tracing on The Wall. It had a cross next to it. "Zorn Miller."

"Who was he?" I asked.

Z had nearly disappeared entirely, except for a sort of shimmering in the air, and his faraway voice, echoing behind him, saying, "Pretty sure it was me."

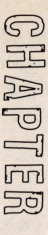

Julie came up behind us a minute later. Greg and I were still standing where Z had left us, dumbfounded.

"Was that Z?" Julie asked.

I looked around to make sure Uncle Dex wasn't with her, and then I nodded.

"And we know his name now," Greg said. "Or at least we're pretty sure we do. And *he's* pretty sure."

"What is it?" Julie asked.

Greg and I both pointed to "Zorn Miller" on The Wall. "He said this was him," I said. "I guess 'Z' for 'Zorn.'"

It was Julie's turn to trace a name on The Wall with her finger. She was quiet for a minute, then she perked up. "We can find out where he died and when he died and everything," she said. "Up the hill where they have the directories. We can find out where he was from, too. His hometown. Your uncle Dex said they have that in the directories as well."

"He's listed as missing," Greg pointed out. "That's what the little cross by his name means. But they never found him, so they just figure he must be dead somewhere."

"But it's a great start," I added. "Where's Uncle Dex, anyway?"

Julie nodded up the hill. "He stayed at the Lincoln Memorial. He said he'd be back in a little while to find us. We should go look up Z in one of the directories before he comes."

It was hard tearing ourselves away from that place at The Wall, even though Zorn Miller wasn't with us anymore, and even though we had all the information we were going to get from being there. Maybe it was the strange way our reflections made us a part of The Wall, and connected us to all those 58,286 names, and all the men and women they represented.

We finally managed to pull ourselves away and trudge up the hill to see what else we could learn about Z.

• • •

The directory was pretty helpful, once we figured out how to use it. Actually, once Uncle Dex rejoined us and showed us how. He explained that the names on the wall were listed chronologically by the date a person either went MIA or died. We pretended we had just picked a name and panel at random — Zorn Miller, panel 39E — and wanted to see what we could find out about him.

"Well, see," said Uncle Dex, flipping some pages. "Since it's panel 39E that means we're looking at soldiers who died or went missing the second week of February 1968. So that was at the height of the war. Most of our soldiers who died in Vietnam were killed that year, and in the years before and after."

"What about our guy?" Greg asked. "What about Zorn Miller?"

I couldn't see Z, but I had a sense that he was there all the same, looking over our shoulders and taking it all in.

Uncle Dex studied the directory some more, flipped some more pages, went back and forth for a couple of minutes. The afternoon sun, meanwhile, slipped behind a dark cloud and we all felt the same autumn chill — judging from the way Greg, Julie, and I all shuddered at the same time.

"You guys getting cold?" Uncle Dex asked, though he didn't wait for an answer because he found Z just then.

"Here he is!" Uncle Dex practically shouted. "Zorn Miller. Missing in Action. Casualty Date: February 14, 1968. Date of Birth: July 28, 1941. Home of Record: Barstow, California. Brand of Service: Army. Rank: Sergeant. Casualty Province: Quang Tri."

It was so much information, all of a sudden, that my head was spinning from trying to take it all in. Julie's brain worked a lot faster than mine, though.

"He was only twenty-seven years old," she said.

Greg shook his head. "I thought he was a lot older," he whispered to me.

"Yeah, I know," I whispered back. "He looked a lot older to me, too."

"What's that?" Uncle Dex asked. He'd heard us, but not what we'd said.

"Oh, nothing," Greg responded. "We were just saying we wondered where that place was and all — Quang Tri. And does it say how he died or anything? Or, I mean, how he went missing, or where exactly he went missing from? Stuff like that?"

"I'm pretty sure Quang Tri was the province in South Vietnam that bordered with North Vietnam during the war," Uncle Dex said. "If I remember my Vietnam geography right. So that would be where the Demilitarized Zone was. And 1968 — that was the worst year of all for the war. There was the Tet Offensive, the My Lai Massacre, the Chicago protests, the Paris peace talks. So much went on that year."

Greg scratched his head. "Uh, I don't think I've ever heard of any of those," he said.

Uncle Dex started to close the directory, but a quick-thinking Julie reached in and bookmarked the Zorn Miller page with her hand.

"I just thought I might take some notes on what we found out about that soldier," she explained, trying her best to look innocent. She pulled out a pen and small notebook, which of course she had with her at all times, and jotted everything down.

Uncle Dex turned his attention back to Greg. "I'm sure it would be interesting to look that all up," he said. "It was a really important year in our history. And in Vietnam's history. You might say it was the year we lost the war, even though the fighting went on for five more."

I felt really excited, thinking about all there was to learn, but I felt really tired, too, thinking about all the work we still needed to do.

"One other big thing from that year," Uncle Dex said. "You're definitely going to want to know more about it if you're interested in the war. And it might have even been where Sergeant Miller went missing in action, because it all happened in Quang Tri Province around that time."

"What was it?" Julie asked, her pen poised over her notebook.

Uncle Dex grinned. "You're quite the reporter, Julie," he said.

"Thank you," Julie replied in her most serious voice. "And that 'other big thing'? You were just saying?"

"The Siege of Khe Sanh," Uncle Dex said, and then he spelled "Khe Sanh" for Julie so she'd have it down accurately in her notes. "The beginning of the end of the war in Vietnam."

CHAPTER 12

We were all over our iPhones

the whole way home from the Vietnam Veterans Memorial —
looking up everything Uncle Dex had mentioned that
happened in 1968.

The Paris peace talks obviously didn't have anything to
do with Zorn Miller, since they took place in France, and the
U.S. delegation and the North Vietnam delegation apparently spent a lot of their time just arguing about the shape
of the table they would sit around. Julie seemed personally
offended by that. "I think they acted like little children," she
said. "And while people were being killed in battles!"

"That's the nature of those sorts of negotiations," Uncle Dex said. "Everybody wants to have the upper hand."

While Julie was getting the lowdown on the Paris peace talks, Greg was looking up My Lai — which Uncle Dex had pronounced "Me Lie." It was a tiny village where some U.S. soldiers killed hundreds of women and children and old people. It was one of the most terrible things that happened in the war, and we all got really upset reading about it over Greg's shoulder. There were these awful, awful pictures of people who had been killed and thrown into a ditch. Some were just babies.

"Why did they do that?" Greg asked out loud, his voice shaking. "We were supposed to be the good guys. I mean, we're *always* supposed to be the good guys. Right?"

Uncle Dex tried to explain, but even he had a hard time with it. "Sometimes things happen in war," he said. "They talk about 'the fog of war,' where it's hard to see clearly what's going on, or what you're supposed to do, or who's your enemy and who's your friend. Even if you believe in what you're doing, and even if you're really brave like most soldiers are, to go into battle, it has to be about the hardest thing to do. People get kind of crazy, or scared, or just angry that their fellow soldiers, their friends, have been hurt or killed, and so they start to think everybody is the enemy. That was the case with some of the men who were responsible for My Lai, or that's what I read, anyway."

"But it even happened to babies, what those soldiers did," Julie said quietly. "There are pictures." We were stuck on the interstate now, in slow-moving traffic — so slow you could probably get out and walk home faster, which is what my dad was always saying about the traffic jams he was in when he commuted to and from his job in DC.

Uncle Dex nodded. "Hard to understand that," he agreed. "I guess it was just that in places in Vietnam you never knew who might be the enemy. It could be an old person or even a child sometimes, carrying a weapon or a bomb or something. That's how guerilla war works. You don't know who your enemy is because the enemy can look just like everybody else."

"But, babies?" Julie said again.

"Yeah, I know," Uncle Dex said. "There's no explaining that, except that those men sort of all went crazy together in a way, from the war, and their officers didn't have the kind of control over them that they were supposed to have, to keep things from getting out of hand like they did."

"What happened to the men who did that?" I asked, worried that Z might have been involved. I didn't think I could help somebody who would ever do something like the massacre.

Uncle Dex kept his eyes on the highway, even though we were still barely moving. "There was a cover-up," he said. "All these high-ranking officers lied about what happened. But an army photographer had taken a lot of pictures, so there was proof. You've already seen some of them, and they're pretty horrifying. A year after the massacre, the truth finally came out and a lot of soldiers and officers had charges against them, but in the end nobody was convicted except this one officer, a lieutenant named William Calley who carried out a lot of the killing and ordered his men to do it, too. He only spent a year or two in jail."

"Wow," said Greg. "War totally stinks."

Uncle Dex agreed, and then we all stopped talking for a while.

After another ten minutes, the traffic picked back up and we gained speed and moved on to other things Uncle Dex had mentioned. The Chicago protests, which I looked up on my iPhone, were these wild demonstrations against the war by antiwar protesters during the 1968 Democratic

National Convention in Chicago. The police arrested a lot of the protesters and conked a bunch of them over the head with their nightsticks, and then there was a famous trial of the protest leaders, called the Chicago Seven. Of course, the violence wasn't anything like what happened at My Lai. Nobody got killed in Chicago.

"My dad talked about the protesters one time," Greg said. "He read something in the newspaper about some that set off some bombs to protest the war and the government and everything. He was still really mad about what they did, even though it was so long ago. It was about the only time he ever mentioned anything about being in Vietnam. He said he wished they would've shipped all the protesters over to the war, and then they'd've see what it was really all about."

Greg seemed kind of worked up telling us that. Julie reached over and patted him on the back for a second. Uncle Dex looked back in the rearview mirror.

"It must have been hard for your dad," he said. "Being in the war and all. Especially knowing not everybody was supporting what he was doing."

Greg just shrugged and said, "Yeah, I guess."

I was beginning to hate this whole Vietnam business.

But we still had our job to do, so I kept reading on my phone and pretty soon found some good news.

"Hey, check this out," I said. "Zorn Miller couldn't have been involved in what happened at My Lai. It happened later that year, after he went missing."

"Yes," Julie said, "and see here — it was also in a different province than Quang Tri, where he went missing. Not that that would have mattered. But still, it is one more thing."

We didn't have time to look up the Tet Offensive and the Siege of Khe Sanh because we were finally at our exit off the interstate. All our brains were tired, and Uncle Dex kept rubbing his head, too. All we'd done was ride in a car, visit the memorial, and then come back home, but it was as if we'd been out in the jungle on patrol ourselves for a week. Sort of.

Greg and Julie said their thanks to Uncle Dex as he let each of them out at their houses, and I watched them trudge up their sidewalks and through their front doors, neither of them so much as looking up or waving as they went inside.

"Looks like it's just you and me, Anderson," Uncle Dex said. "And I don't know about you, but I've had about enough of Vietnam for one day."

I was just about to say, "Me too," when I realized Z was sitting next to me in the backseat — or at least a faint, flickering version of him was — staring out the window at first, and then turning to look at me.

He started to say something — I think it was just to thank me for making the trip to The Wall, but maybe some things were starting to come back to him since finding out his name, and when he'd gone missing and all of that.

But then Uncle Dex pulled up in front of my house — just two blocks from Greg's — and Z disappeared.

"Here you go, Anderson," Uncle Dex said. "Say hi to your mom and dad for me."

"Thanks for taking us today," I said, echoing Julie and Greg. "I really learned a lot."

"I'm glad," Uncle Dex said. He turned to look back at me and got a serious look on his face. "Are you okay, Anderson?" he asked. "You seem like something's bothering you. Was it all that we talked about in the car about the war?"

"Yeah," I said, opening the door and climbing out. "I guess so. Anyway, thanks again."

I couldn't exactly say it to Uncle Dex, but the truth was I felt bad because here we all got to quit at the end of the day, but Zorn Miller was still in Vietnam in a way, and he'd been stuck there for most of the past fifty years. He'd probably had enough of it, too, but unless we found a lot more answers for him, and soon, he wasn't ever going to get to go home.

CHAPTER 13

Z didn't show up again after Uncle Dex dropped me off — at least not for a while. Mom wasn't feeling well from her MS, so she stayed in bed during dinner. Dad and I had soup and sandwiches, and he also made me eat some carrot sticks so I would be healthy, or that's what he said. Carrots are what parents give you if they can't remember the last time you ate a vegetable and they're feeling guilty about not feeding you right.

"So what's on the agenda for tonight?" Dad asked. I had almost forgotten it was Saturday — not that I ever did much on Saturday nights, or any night, really. It wasn't like I got invited to a lot of cool parties. But then I remembered.

"There's an All-Ages Concert," I said. "Do you think it would be okay if I called Greg to see if he can go?

Dad dunked a corner of his grilled cheese into his tomato soup and took a soggy bite. It did not look appetizing. "Is your band playing?" he asked. "What's the name again — the Spirits of War?"

"The *Ghosts* of War," I corrected him. "And no, we're not playing. That's next weekend, the next open mic night they're having. But we haven't practiced nearly enough to be ready for that."

Dad switched over to a soup spoon. "Well, I'm sure that would be all right if you and Greg wanted to go," he said. "Do you know anything about the band that *is* playing?"

"Not really," I said. "Just that it's not us and it's not Belman's band, either."

"Who?" Dad asked. I guess I hadn't told him much about Belman, but now probably wasn't the time. If I explained about what a bully Belman was, Dad might not let us go to the concert.

"Just this guy at school," I said. "His band is, like, our main number one rival. At the open mic night." That wasn't technically true — Belman's band was about a hundred times better than the Ghosts of War — but at the same time it was kind of true.

·   ·   ·

Greg was happy that I called him.

"Definitely," he said. "When can you pick me up? Actually, never mind. I'll just come on over to your house."

I could tell from the way his voice sounded that things probably weren't too good with his dad, and turns out I was right. He was so ready to get out of his house that he must have been running over to mine while we were still on the phone, because it seemed like not even a minute later he was knocking on the front door.

He told me what was going on while we waited for my dad to get ready so he could drive us to the concert.

"Stupid me," he said. "I went ahead and asked my dad about Vietnam when I got home and he got kind of mad about it. Well, not mad exactly, but just really tense, the way he does sometimes. Usually he goes and gets a drink when that happens."

"What did you ask him?"

Greg kind of scuffed his shoes on the mat just inside our front door. "Just, like, was he in Vietnam in 1968, and how old was he, and where was he. Stuff like that."

"I guess he didn't answer you?" I said.

"No," Greg said. "I mean, yes. The funny thing is he *did* answer me. He said he was twenty-two and yeah, he was there in '68, and he said I probably never heard of where he'd been and then he just said it was in the north, in the jungle mostly."

"Anything else?" I asked.

"Not really," Greg said. "Just that he was in the army, and he was a Green Beret, like in that song."

"Wouldn't it be crazy if he knew Z?" I asked.

"Yeah," Greg said. "Wonder if they might have ever met each other? *That* would have been crazy."

"We could ask," I said.

"No," Greg said, shaking his head pretty emphatically. "I already asked too much as it is. I bet Dad's already opening his fourth beer by now."

We heard my dad in the kitchen just then, grabbing his keys off the hook. "You boys ready to go?" he half shouted down the hall.

"Yes, Dad," I half shouted back.

"Yes, Mr. Carter," Greg added. He was always super polite when it came to my parents.

"So what happened next with your dad?" I asked Greg.

"Nothing," he said. "That was all he said, and then he got a beer. And then he got kind of cranky and you called and I figured it was time to go."

·　　·　　·

We were halfway to the place where they held the all-ages concerts — this drum store called Eyeclops that had a big warehouse in back — when Julie called my cell phone. "Do you and Greg want to go to the concert?" she asked. "I was trying to do more research, but I am overwhelmed by so much happening today and already learning so much about Zorn Miller and Vietnam."

I felt guilty that we hadn't asked her to come with us, so I sort of lied and didn't tell her we were already on our way there. Instead, I said that was a great idea and my brain was tired, too, and I asked if she wanted us to pick her up.

"That would be very nice," she said. "Thank you. I'll be waiting."

"Oops," Greg said after I hung up. He had listened in on the conversation.

"Yeah, I know," I said, and then I asked Dad if he could make an extra stop on the way.

·　　·　　·

The concert was great — at first. The band was called the Dismemberment Plan and they were four older guys from Washington, DC, but they were still really good, and really loud, and their songs had really cool titles, like "Daddy Was a Real Good Dancer," and "Spider in the Snow," and "Girl O'Clock." They even had one called "Bra," which Greg and I couldn't stop laughing about. Julie just rolled her eyes at us.

Then this kid came up and asked her if she wanted to dance. He was a sixth grader like us, a big-time gamer named Quinn who wore really thick glasses, probably because he wrecked his eyesight staring at pixels so much. That was the story about him, anyway. He was about six inches shorter than Julie.

She looked at me, then at Greg. Then, when neither one of us could think of anything to say, she nodded at Quinn and off they went to dance together. Quinn was a really good dancer. Julie kind of worked hard to keep up with him.

Greg and I just stood and stared.

"Uh, I wasn't expecting that to happen," he said.

I actually felt kind of, well, weird. Or something. Not that I was about to say anything to Greg — and definitely not to Julie.

"Yeah," I said, because I had no clue what else to say.

Fortunately, the song was really short, and when it ended Julie said something to Quinn, then she came back over to me and Greg. I don't think we'd so much as shuffled our feet the whole time she was gone.

"Tomorrow we will get serious about practicing again," she said, as if what had just happened was no big deal.

Greg said, "Definitely," and I said, "Totally," and then the band started up again and the next thing I knew the crowd swelled around us and everybody was jumping up and down so we started jumping up and down with the rest of the kids. It was a song called "Invisible Man."

Halfway through, though, somebody crashed into me and sent me crashing into Greg and both of us went sprawling across the dance floor. I skinned my elbow and got blood on my sleeve. Greg rubbed his head and seemed woozy. The music kept going, but a couple of the adult chaperones waded through the crowd of kids and dragged us outside into the waiting area where parents hung out.

One of them handed Greg an ice pack, and another taped gauze over my wounded arm.

I thought they'd be sympathetic, but they weren't.

"If you boys can't behave, then you won't be allowed to come back," this one lady said.

"But we didn't do anything," I said. "Somebody ran into us."

"Then you need to be sure you get out of the way next time," said a man with big glasses and a ponytail, even though his hair was mostly gone on top. He was a little friendlier than the lady, at least.

"Sorry," Greg said, even though we really didn't have anything to apologize for.

The man and the lady left us sitting there on a sagging couch and went back inside. Julie came out when they went in.

"Are you guys okay?" she asked. "I can't believe they did that!"

I shrugged. "They're just doing their job, I guess, being chaperones."

"Not them," Julie said. "Didn't you see who ran into you and Greg?"

Greg and I both shook our heads.

Julie made a noise that actually sounded like growling. "It was Belman," she said. "He and his friends just showed up.

They were banging into everybody on the dance floor, and then when they saw you guys they acted like it was the funniest thing in the world to knock you down. Like bowling."

"You saw it all?" I asked. "Weren't you dancing with that kid again — with Quinn?"

"No," Julie said, with this sort of shy smile. "Anyway, he was dancing with somebody else. I think he's what they call a player."

"You mean a gamer?" I asked. "He plays a lot of computer games."

Julie shrugged. "That, too. But also a player. He dances with a lot of girls. That's all."

I decided to let it go before I made a total fool out of myself for pressing things about Julie dancing with Quinn.

"What do we do now?" I asked. "I mean, should we go back in? I'm just kind of wondering if Belman and his friends might knock into us again if we do."

And Quinn might ask Julie to dance again. But I just thought that; I didn't say it out loud.

Julie growled again. "We should report them."

"No," Greg said. "It would just be our word against theirs. And anyway, my head hurts and I think I want to go home."

It was my turn to growl.

CHAPTER 14

Greg stayed over at my house that night. He fell asleep pretty much right away once Dad brought us home and Greg dragged out his usual sleeping bag from under my bed. I was wide-awake, though, my brain spinning with all the stuff that had happened that day.

Of course I kept thinking about The Wall and finding out Z's real name, plus when he went missing in Vietnam, and where anybody last saw him, or sort of where, anyway. They had it narrowed down to the province, so at least we had that to go on. All kinds of other things, too: his rank and his hometown. Maybe tomorrow we could try to get in touch with anybody who knew him. Maybe he had a wife and kids. Maybe check out a Vietnam veterans' website. There were probably a bunch of those, where guys stayed in touch with one another, and where they posted stuff about guys who didn't make it back from the war. There were all sorts of possibilities.

I felt kind of bad that I had gone out to the concert when probably I should have stayed home and followed up on all these new leads. And with the clock ticking on how long we had to solve Z's mystery for him, what had I been thinking? Of course I should have stayed home. Just one more thing to feel guilty about, I guess.

Plus, not inviting Julie to go with Greg and me. That wasn't exactly the nicest thing, either. And I couldn't quite figure out why it made me feel so weird when Julie danced with Quinn. I mean, it wasn't like *I* wanted to dance with her. But that didn't mean I wanted Quinn to. I sighed.

And then there was that big jerk Belman. I wished I knew what to do about him. It seemed like every time I turned around, there he was making life difficult for us.

I was just stewing over all this stuff, unable to turn my thoughts off, when a sort of shadow appeared at the end of my bed. That's the best way I can describe it.

"You're looking kind of down there, son," a voice said from that direction. "Been quite a day, huh?"

Z was back! I was already sitting up on my bed. "Yeah," I said. "I mean, yes, sir."

He laughed. "I'm not an officer," he said. "Just a sergeant. At least according to that big headstone you took me to today. The Wall. You don't call me 'sir.' Just a 'Yes, Sergeant' will do."

"Yes, Sergeant," I said.

"So look," he said. "I appreciate all you kids have done for me. I'm still putting it all together, what we found out today, but I just want you to know. You all have been a big help. I'm glad you went out tonight and had you some fun. Don't feel bad about that. You deserved it. Even if it didn't end up so great."

I didn't know what to say. It was almost as if Z — Sergeant Miller — had been reading my mind or something. And as if he'd been there at the concert keeping an eye on us. Too bad he couldn't have done something about Belman. Maybe just haunt the guy a little, give him a good ghost scare. And maybe trip Quinn while he was at it.

It was Greg who responded to Z this time. "Thanks," he

said from somewhere inside his sleeping bag. We must have woken him up.

"And all that business you kids were talking about in the car," Z continued. "Sounded like some hard stuff. Wasn't anything I heard about before, but things happen in war like your uncle said — things that aren't supposed to happen but they do, and you can't always know the reasons. That doesn't mean everybody ought to get away with doing whatever they want. I'm not saying that. Criminal stuff like what happened at My Lai, you can't let that sort of thing go. You have to hold people accountable, you know? But you have to forgive people, too. At least some. And you have to forgive yourself for some of the things you have to do. That's all I'm saying."

We were all quiet for a minute until I said, "Yes, sir. I mean, yes, Sergeant."

Greg asked another question. "Is there anything else you can remember, since we found out who you are and all? I mean, like where you happened to end up being missing in the war."

"Yeah," I joined in. "And were you married or anything like that?"

"And who's Fish?" Greg added.

"Not so fast," Z said, waving his hands — and his unlit cigar with the chewed-up end. "And yeah, actually there is something."

He paused, like he was collecting his thoughts together, and then he let out what sounded like a deep breath, though I guess ghosts don't exactly breathe.

"There was Philomena," he said. "And the nugget. When I saw my name there on The Wall, and then where I was from, it got me thinking about what else was back there — or rather *who* else. And so it came to me — their names and all."

"Philomena?" Greg asked.

"The nugget?" I asked.

"Right," he said. "My wife. And last I knew, she was pregnant. In our letters we took to calling the baby 'the nugget' since we didn't know if it was a girl or boy yet."

"Which one was it?" I asked. "I mean, once it was born."

"Never got to find out," Z said. "Philomena was probably about seven months along when I, well, you know."

Z's voice had picked up a sad echo, and it was already fading out, too, getting fainter with each word so I had to strain to hear the last thing he said. I was pretty sure I'd heard him right, though — about Philomena and the nugget and all.

"We'll find her for you," Greg said, as the rest of Z faded out, too. "I promise."

And then Z was gone.

"Greg!" I said. "You can't promise something like that. I mean, we can try, but there are a lot of people out there, and all we know is where Z was from, but not his wife and stuff."

"Yeah, but how many Philomenas can there be in the world?" Greg asked.

Hundreds, as it turned out, thanks to a quick Internet search, the last thing we did before both Greg and I collapsed into sleep that night.

But only one Philomena Miller who lived in Barstow, California.

CHAPTER 15

Julie came over early the next morning. I'm not sure where she got the idea to do it, but there she was all of a sudden, tapping on my bedroom window to wake us up. It was Sunday morning, and we were totally zonked out from staying up so late the night before talking to Z and then looking up Philomena Miller.

Fortunately, she brought donuts, so we let her in.

"I stayed up practically all night," she said as Greg and I scarfed down a couple of glazed donuts each before we said a word.

"Hold on," I said, or mumbled, through a mouth full of donut. "Gotta get some milk."

I ran out of my bedroom and down the hall to the kitchen. Mom and Dad were sitting at the table, drinking coffee and reading the paper.

"Are you feeling better, Mom?" I asked, though I didn't slow down on my way to the refrigerator. I grabbed a gallon jug of milk and some cups and swung back around.

"Yes, sweetie," she said. "Where are you going with that milk?"

"Julie brought donuts," I said as I swept back out of the kitchen. "Gotta go."

"Wait!" Dad yelled after me. "How did she get in?"

"Window!" I yelled back, as if it was the most natural thing in the world. With Greg I guess it was, and Mom and Dad were used to that. So probably that explained why all they said about Julie coming in that way, too, was "Oh. Well, tell her we said hi."

Back in my room, I poured us each a cup of milk. Greg and I, acting like we were totally starving, speared more donuts, though I did manage to ask Julie what she was doing up all night before I took another giant bite of mine.

"*Almost* all night," she corrected me. "And please will you eat with your mouth closed? Anyway, I was on the Internet, of course. Doing research."

"What did you find out?" Greg asked. " 'Cause we did some research, too, and we found out a bunch of things. Like Z's wife's name was —"

"Philomena!" Julie interrupted. "It was Philomena. And he had a son, too. And the son also has an unusual name."

"What?" I asked. I had parked yet another donut on my index finger and was taking bites around the outside, working my way in to the middle.

"Nugent," Julie said. "Nugent Miller."

"You mean Nugget," Greg corrected her.

"No, no," said Julie. "Not Nugget. Nugent."

Greg and I cracked up laughing. "That's too funny," I said. "Z told us last night that when his wife was pregnant they didn't know if it was a boy or a girl so they just called it the nugget. Z went missing before the baby was born. His wife must have found a real name that was closest to that — to nugget — and given that name to the baby."

"So, Nugget, Nugent," Julie said, shaking her head. "How strange."

"You mean how perfect!" Greg said, still laughing.

"Nugent, huh?" said another voice in the room. "Gonna take some time to get used to that one, but I think I like it, too."

We all turned to look at Z, in his usual place on the floor at the end of my bed, his back to the wall, contemplating that cigar. I was glad to see him back so soon.

"Uh, congratulations?" said Greg.

"Yeah, uh, congratulations," I echoed. "It's a boy!"

Z shook his head. "Well, what do you know about that?" he asked nobody in particular. "So I'm a dad. Or I was a dad. Or I could have been a dad. Or whatever."

I turned back to Julie. "How did you find out?" I asked.

She waved her hand as if to say it was no big deal. "Online records," she said, adding, "Also, I have a phone number that we can call once it gets a little later in California."

I didn't tell her that we had found that out, too, and neither did Greg. Best to let her think all that work she'd done, and staying up most of the night, was worth it.

But there was more.

"Sergeant Miller," she said to Z, who was still shaking his head over the news about Nugent, and pretty obviously wishing he could light up his cigar for real — this time to celebrate. "I also found out where you went missing, and it was one of the places that Anderson's uncle mentioned yesterday in the car."

Z looked up, his face a big question mark.

"Khe Sanh," she said.

Z's expression didn't change, not right away. He still had that quizzical look on his face, staring at Julie as if waiting for her to say more, and then he seemed to be gazing at something else a long ways away, even though he was still just sitting there on the floor in my bedroom at the end of my bed.

"What is going on?" Julie whispered to Greg and me.

"I'm not sure," I said. "Maybe it's what you told him about having a son. Or maybe it's about Khe Sanh. Or maybe it's both."

"It's the thousand-yard stare," Greg said.

"What's that?" Julie asked.

"It's this thing my mom explained to me," Greg said. "I've seen my dad do it and I asked her about it one time. She said she guessed it had something to do with being in combat and stuff. People who have been there, like my dad, they just kind of space out sometimes and get that look on their faces like they're staring at something a thousand yards away, only they're not really staring at anything the rest of us can see. She said in the war guys got that way a lot, too, because of what they'd seen and had to do, and also how exhausted they were from the patrols they had to go on and how stressful all that was. Sometimes Dad would stay like that for a long time, even when you were trying to talk to him and ask him questions. It used to be really hard for my mom to handle things like that about my dad."

I'd never heard Greg say so much about his family, definitely not all in one breath like that. I didn't know what to say to him, and we all just sat in silence for a minute. But Julie knew what to do. She was really kind and all and patted him on the shoulder, which was this thing she always did instead of maybe hugging somebody when she wanted to make them feel better.

"So maybe he is remembering stuff," I said hopefully, turning the conversation back to Z. "About Khe Sanh and all."

"It was a terrible battle," Julie said. "I read a lot about it already. It was really a siege."

"Which is what exactly?" I asked. "Like when knights of old laid siege to a castle?"

"You mean surrounded it?" Greg asked. "And they would raise the drawbridge so the knights couldn't get across, and they had moats and stuff like that?"

"Yes," Julie said. "Except there wasn't a castle. And instead of a moat, they had concertina wire, which is like barbed wire, surrounding the camp at Khe Sanh. It was a marine base, near a village called Khe Sanh, very near the border to North Vietnam."

"The DMZ?" Greg asked.

"Yes," said Julie. "Just south of the DMZ. And it was a narrow part of Vietnam so very near the border with the country of Laos to the west, as well, and very near the ocean to the east. There were mountains. Or hills, anyway. The Central Highlands."

"So who sieged who?" Greg asked.

Julie rolled her eyes. Her sympathy for Greg didn't last too long, I guess. "That's not a word. And also it's 'whom,' not 'who.'"

"Huh?" Greg said.

Julie sighed this time. "What you should have said was 'Who laid siege to whom?'"

"Okay," Greg said, as sarcastically as he could.

Julie did not like that at all. "Fine, then," she said. "Look it up for yourselves. And I'll take my donuts back, too."

I looked at the empty donut box. "Uh, yeah, maybe not," I said. "We sort of already ate them all. And Greg's sorry. He didn't mean anything. Right, Greg?"

Greg apologized, too, which was enough for Julie. She

started to tell us more about the Battle of Khe Sanh or the Siege of Khe Sanh or whatever it was supposed to be called, when we realized that Z wasn't there anymore. I had no idea when he'd vanished this time.

"All that thousand-yard staring must have worn him out," Greg said.

"Perhaps," said Julie. "Is that happening more often? That he doesn't stay for very long when he is here, when he shows himself and speaks to you?"

"Yeah," I said. "I think so."

"I was afraid of that," she said.

I was afraid of it, too.

CHAPTER 16

We had to split up to go to church since it was Sunday and since we all went to different ones. Mom, Dad, and I usually attended the Methodist church, Greg went to a Presbyterian church where his dad dropped him off but didn't stay himself, and Julie was a half Buddhist, half Catholic, so she went to a Unitarian Universalist church where she said you could believe anything you wanted. I couldn't see that there was much difference between Methodist and Presbyterian, from what Greg told me.

Just before she left, Julie told us we had to meet her at the downtown library right after church so we could do more research.

"I thought we were going to call Z's wife," Greg said.

"Yes," said Julie. "We will call Z's wife. But you guys should know at least *something* about Khe Sanh, since that's where he went missing."

"Okay," I said. "The library first. But what are we going to tell Mrs. Miller when we call? And who's calling this time? I did it last time."

"I think Julie should do it," Greg said.

"Fine," Julie said with a shake of her head.

"So what do we tell her?" I asked again. "If she even answers the phone."

Julie bit on her lip for a second, then had an idea. "We tell her we're in middle school and we're working on a project about The Wall and we wanted to look up family members and other people who knew someone whose name we found on The Wall. And we found Zorn Miller's name and that's why we're calling — to see if she'd be willing to talk to us about him."

"You mean like what exactly happened to him in the war?" I asked. "Or do you mean like who was he and all before he went to the war?"

"Both," Julie said. "If she knows both."

•　　•　　•

We were too late for Sunday school, and Mom wasn't feeling well again anyway, so it was just me and Dad who went to church after Julie and Greg left. Dad was an usher so he was busy greeting and helping to seat people. Which meant I got to sit by myself for a while, until after the ushers took up the offering.

We sang a couple of hymns, which I always like since I actually do like singing — I was just still not so sure about being the singer for the Ghosts of War. And then I pulled out my iPhone and hid it between pages of the hymnal so I could look up Khe Sanh. I didn't want to have to wait to get to the library to get started. Wikipedia seemed as good a place to start as anywhere. Not that Julie had to know that.

One thing I found out was that the marines knew for months that the North Vietnamese Army was planning something big at Khe Sanh, and they were pretty sure it was going to be a massive attack on the base. They had all kinds of intelligence sources that told them stuff, and the marine patrols in that area also could tell that something was going on.

The crazy thing was that the U.S. generals weren't even sure they needed a marine base at Khe Sanh, and most of them talked about just abandoning it rather than defending it.

There were a bunch of NVA divisions moving into the Central Highlands — NVA stood for North Vietnamese Army — and they were mostly hiding out just over the border in Laos, where the Americans weren't allowed to go because the U.S. Congress didn't want the war to get any bigger and more spread out than it already was just in Vietnam. Another reason for that was because the war was getting more and more unpopular as the U.S. and South Vietnam kept not winning, but U.S. military guys kept getting wounded and killed.

So anyway, everybody knew the NVA was getting ready to attack, they just didn't know when, until this one marine patrol caught an NVA soldier and he told them it was going to be near the end of January 1968. It was late in 1967 when they found this out, so there was still plenty of time to just shut down the base and leave. No real good reason to keep it open, especially since it would be difficult to bring in reinforcements, plus the base was pretty much a big zero in terms of keeping the NVA from slipping into South Vietnam or sending supplies and weapons to the Viet Cong, their guerilla fighters down in the south. The North Vietnamese guys just stayed on the Laos side of the border and brought guns and everything down this big hidden dirt highway called the Ho Chi Minh Trail, which was named after the leader of North Vietnam, Ho Chi Minh.

But General William Westmoreland, who was the commander of all the U.S. military in Vietnam, ordered Khe Sanh to stay open, kind of because he didn't believe in backing down from a fight, or something like that, which meant that the marines were just sitting ducks. There were six thousand of them stuck on the base with nowhere to go. They were surrounded by thirty thousand North Vietnamese troops, all dug in, with lots and lots of artillery.

That was as far as I got before Dad came and joined me at my pew, a little while after the ushers took up the offering and brought it back to the church office. I had to quickly shut down my phone, but I knew I wasn't quick enough because of the stern look Dad gave me when he sat down.

"So what was that you were doing on your phone during church today?" Dad asked as we were driving home.

"Oh," I said. "Nothing. Just, you know, something Julie said I should read."

"Love letter?" Dad asked.

I nearly jumped out of my seat. "No!" I shouted. "I mean,

no way! Julie's not my girlfriend or anything. She's just in the band."

Dad laughed. "Take it easy there," he said. "But whatever it was, next time let's pay attention during the service. Got it?"

"Yes, Dad," I said. "Sorry. It was just — it was kind of important. That's all."

Dad patted me on the shoulder. "I'm sure it was," he said, in that kind of voice grown-ups use when what they mean is that because you're a kid, how important could it really be?

Boy, did I ever wish I could tell him.

• • •

Julie, Greg, and I met up at the library later that afternoon. Actually, Julie was already there — no surprise — and she had a stack of books out for us to read. Fortunately for Greg, who wasn't a great reader, one of them was a giant book of photographs from the war, with a whole section on the Siege of Khe Sanh.

"You're late," Julie said before either of us even got a chance to say hello.

"We got here as soon as we could, Your Majesty," Greg said.

I thought Julie would get crabby at the way he said that, but instead she just made this sort of royal hand gesture at us, like we were her subjects, and said, "Uneasy lies the head that wears the crown."

Then she smiled and said, "Shakespeare."

Greg didn't miss a beat. "Who's he?"

That made Julie scowl. Greg grinned. But then we got down to business.

Julie assigned me and her a couple of regular books — one a pretty standard history book and the other one a first-person account of the siege by a guy who was there. She got the first one, I got the second, and we spent the next couple of hours poring over our books, every now and then one of us telling the others about something we read or saw. Greg had the picture book and he did the most interrupting and sharing with his photos. Some of them — the ones of men who'd been killed or wounded — were pretty hard to look at.

• • •

Together, we found out a ton about the Siege of Khe Sanh. It was on January 21, 1968, when the battle actually started. The marines were just sitting on the base, doing their regular stuff at three in the morning — most of them sleeping —

when the North Vietnamese Army attacked a marine outpost on a hill overlooking the base. Two hours later, this terrible barrage of about three hundred bombs rained down on the base. One scored a direct hit on the main ammunition dump. Greg showed us a photo of the explosion, which was enormous.

The NVA divisions had a ton of hidden artillery, including a bunch of cannons in caves in the mountains, and that's where they were firing from. Nobody knew how they'd been able to sneak all that artillery into place. The next afternoon, helicopters, sort of a rescue force, were sent from somewhere to the base to carry out wounded men and to bring more ammunition, but the NVA were waiting and opened fire and shot down most of the helicopters when they tried to land. There were pictures of the downed helicopters, too.

Eighteen marines were killed that first day.

And that was just the beginning. The bombings kept up, and didn't stop — for seventy-seven days! Julie's book said the North Vietnamese wanted to force the marines out of their base so they would be easier to attack. They blew up the ammunition dump and kept attacking the perimeter of the base and observation outposts all around the base, and for weeks, any time a U.S. helicopter tried to land to bring in more supplies or ammo, or to take away killed and wounded marines, the NVA shot it down, too.

The roads were closed, all bridges had been blown up.

Nobody could get in, and nobody could get out.

The marines fought off every attack on their perimeter, and there were air strikes on the NVA positions almost constantly — or what they suspected were NVA positions. One problem was the NVA cannons in those caves. They were on tracks, so the NVA could roll them out and fire a bunch of shells into the base and onto the marines. But before the marines could trace the trajectory of the bombs and locate the cannons — and order air force bombers flying over from an aircraft carrier just off the coast to hit those targets — the North Vietnamese would just roll them back inside the caves and camouflage the openings, and then they would roll them out again. They did this at random times over the course of the day, so the marines never knew when to expect an attack.

The NVA dug trenches and tunnels to get closer and closer to the marine base — working like crazy all night. They also kept attacking marine outposts on high hills that overlooked the base, and the NVA had so many more men that a lot of the marines in those outposts ran out of ammunition and had to fight hand to hand with their fists and knives. The guy I read about had been in one of those outposts, and had been in these really awful hand-to-hand combats. It was hard to read about how many of his friends got killed, and how much he missed them.

One account told of nearly fifty men who were killed when the transport plane they were on — trying to bring them in as reinforcements — was shot down by the NVA with heavy machine gun and recoilless rifle fire. Greg showed us the picture. Nobody survived.

And as the siege wore on, even more men were killed. A lot more. As many as a thousand marines and other U.S. soldiers died in all.

CHAPTER 17

When we finally left the library, all three of us just sat on the steps outside in the sun, just sort of in a daze, blinking, not saying anything at first. That seemed to be happening a lot lately.

"I wonder if Z is remembering any of this on his own?" Greg finally asked.

"Too bad he's not here with us now," I said. "You know, reading over our shoulders or whatever."

Julie nodded. "But we should go. We have a phone call to make, and it's getting late in the afternoon."

Five minutes later, we were at the Kitchen Sink, upstairs at the counter, since it was Sunday and Uncle Dex wouldn't be in, and because none of our phones worked in the basement too well.

"Do you think she'll be mad at us?" Greg asked.

"Why would she be angry?" Julie replied. "We're not trying to sell her anything, or say anything that she wouldn't want to hear."

"Well, she might be mad at us for calling because maybe she hasn't thought about him in a long time," I said. "And, you know, maybe she doesn't want to have to think about something that was so painful and all. Or talk about it."

"To strangers," Greg added.

"Yeah," I said. "Kid strangers."

Julie tapped her cell phone on her chin for a minute. Then she said, "Maybe. Or maybe she will appreciate that even so long after the war, that someone — us — is still interested in what happened to her husband, and what happened to her. What she suffered in losing him. And raising her son, the nugget, by herself."

"Nugent," Greg corrected her, even though it was Julie who'd actually found out the name.

Julie narrowed her eyes and gave him a look. "I'll make the call," she said. "You two can just listen."

"Mind if I listen in, too?" It was Z, suddenly there standing next to us.

"You scared me," Greg said, laughing nervously.

"Me too," I said, though I'd sort of been expecting him — or hoping he'd show up, anyway.

"Of course," said Julie, already dialing. It felt like I held my breath forever while we waited to see who would answer, and what she'd say. Greg must have held his breath, too, because I could see his face getting really red. Z studied the unlit end of his cigar.

It went to voice mail. "Hello. This is Philomena Miller. Not home right now, but you can leave a message. And if you're a burglar checking out the place to see if anybody's here, you should know that I have two big dogs just sitting next to the door waiting for the likes of you to ever show up."

I just about swallowed my tongue, but Julie kept her cool. "Hi, Mrs. Miller," she said. "My name is Julie Kobayashi, and my friends and I are calling because we were hoping it would be okay to talk to you about Sergeant Zorn Miller. It's for a school project about Vietnam. And we apologize if we're bothering you and you would rather not speak with us. Thank you, and here's my number if you want to call us back."

Julie left her number and hung up.

We all just stood there for a minute. I was wondering if Z recognized his wife's voice.

He did.

"That's her all right," he said softly, and then he whistled. "Haven't heard that voice in a long, long time."

"So she sounds the same?" Greg asked.

"Little bit older," Z said. "Guess she'd be a lot older, from what you all have told me about what year this is."

"Are you okay?" I asked. "I mean, is it weird, or hard, or whatever, to hear her like that?"

Z smiled. "Kind of nice, really," he said.

We all just stood around for a while, waiting, hoping we'd get a call back right away, but that didn't happen. Julie filled Z in on everything we'd learned about the Siege of Khe Sanh, and he listened intently the whole time she talked, but when she finished he didn't say much.

"Kind of fuzzy," he said. "Gonna have to let it all sink in, see if it'll come into focus. Something tells me maybe I wasn't around for most of it."

"Well, actually, you weren't," Julie said, kind of apologetically. "The date when you went missing — it was just a few weeks after the beginning of the siege."

Z nodded but didn't say anything. Then I guess he got tired of us standing there just staring at him, waiting to see if he remembered anything else, because he suggested we go ahead with band practice.

"You kids could use a little more rehearsal time," he said. He nodded at me. "Break in your new singer here."

"Yeah," I said. "About that . . ."

Julie sniffed. "Well, if you don't want me," she said. "And if it can't be Greg anymore, which it can't . . ." She didn't finish.

We went downstairs for our instruments and brought them upstairs, then ran through what Julie called our "standards" — that one song about bullying that she wrote, "Monkey See, Monkey Do," and that other one she wrote about a hamster called "Hamster Talks." I had a hard time matching my voice to the key we'd been playing them in when Greg was our singer. Z, who was actually managing to stick around longer for once, had a good laugh about that, and it made me happy that he was staying around. He'd been fading out so quickly lately, and not showing up at all sometimes, that I'd been worried we were already losing him and running out of time. Maybe it was being so close to us while we were talking to his wife, and finding out more

· 131 ·

about what happened to him, that was keeping him around longer today.

I did a lot better when we switched keys. Julie had to coach Greg and me on the new chord progression, of course. Greg must have been doing a lot more practicing than me because he was playing a little bit of the melody on his guitar while I did my regular strumming. Naturally, Julie didn't have any trouble on the keyboards.

"I like it," Z announced when we finished.

"Which song?" Julie asked.

Z shrugged. "Both. Anderson there has a sweet voice, and those are some nice songs."

I wasn't so sure I liked being described that way — as sweet — and it made me anxious all over again at the thought of being the lead singer for the Ghosts of War at the next All-Ages Open Mic Night.

Julie suggested we try one of the Dismemberment Plan songs, which she'd obviously been thinking about because she had already prepared sheet music for us, with the chords and lyrics and everything. It was that song of theirs called "Girl O'Clock." We muddled through it for half an hour, me and Greg messing up repeatedly while Julie did her usual sighs of exasperation at us.

Toward the end, I noticed Z flickering in and out, that staticky thing that happened when he stopped being stable or whatever.

Greg saw it, too. "Don't go! She might call!" he shouted, as if that might stop the disappearing process, and as if Z hadn't already stayed with us so much longer than usual.

And then, as if on cue, Julie's phone rang. She froze when she looked at the number.

"California!" she said. "It's the number I called for Mrs. Miller."

"Well, answer it already!" Greg urged.

So she did. Greg and I pressed in close so we could hear. Somehow Z managed to stay with us, too, though he kept fading in and out so much that it was hard for me to see his face and how hearing everything might be affecting him.

"Hello?" Julie said. "This is Julie."

"The young lady who called earlier?" a woman's voice asked.

"Yes," Julie said. "That was me. Are you Mrs. Miller? Mrs. Philomena Miller?"

"I am," the lady said. "And Zorn Miller was my husband."

Julie took a deep breath, and then continued, "I hope you don't mind that we have called," she said. "To ask about Sergeant Miller. We are very sorry for your loss."

"Thank you," Mrs. Miller said. "It was a long time ago, but we still miss him. Every day."

"Do you mind if we ask you some things about him and about Vietnam?" Julie asked.

Mrs. Miller hesitated for a long time, so long I almost thought she'd hung up on us, but then she responded. "No, I suppose not. And you said in your message that this was for a school project."

"Well, yes. Sort of," Julie said. "We visited the Vietnam Veterans Memorial and we found Sergeant Miller's name. And they had information there at The Wall about him and where he was from, and that's how we found you."

"Not so hard to do that," Mrs. Miller said. "I still live in the same town. I still live in the same house, too. And I never remarried. I suppose you already know that since you got hold of me here."

"And you have a son?" Julie asked. "He must be grown now."

"Yes," Mrs. Miller said. "He joined the army like his

father. But he didn't join Special Forces. He's a helicopter pilot, stationed at Fort Campbell, in Kentucky."

"I'm sure his father would be very proud of him," Julie said, sounding like a grown-up herself.

I turned to Z and saw his face then, just for a second, and he did look proud. Not smiling exactly, but almost tearful, except not in a bad way.

Apparently, he wasn't the only one feeling that way just then. Mrs. Miller started to say something else but choked up. "I'm sorry," she said. "I told myself I wouldn't start crying, that I would just answer your questions. I really do appreciate that you and your friends care enough to want to know about my husband — about Zorn. Not very many people care about our veterans — those who are still living or the ones like my husband who didn't come back."

Julie couldn't speak all of a sudden and I looked at her to see why.

She was crying now, too.

CHAPTER 18

Once Mrs. Miller got started talking she kept going for quite a while. She told us all about how she and Z met in high school. "I know it's a silly cliché," she said. "But he was on the football team and I was a cheerleader. Only he wasn't a quarterback or anything. I'm not sure he ever actually got into a game, to tell you the truth. He was pretty scrawny in high school. Wasn't until he joined the army that he grew and filled out. All that exercise, all those drills. Plus, he just got his growth spurt kind of late."

I thought I heard Z sort of chuckle when she said that, but it could have just been a random noise. He was almost all the way flickering out when I turned again to look, though he still didn't disappear altogether. I could tell he was working really, really hard to stick around for our conversation with his wife.

"Z had already done two tours in Vietnam when he applied for the Green Berets," Mrs. Miller said. "He never talked much about those tours. He just seemed so frustrated with the whole thing, but he thought it was his duty to keep going back. At first it was about doing his duty as an American, and fighting communism, but after a while it seemed to be more about his feeling that he needed to be there to protect his men. He felt so guilty when he was back in the States and they were still over there in Vietnam. He thought Special Forces — that's the real name for the Green Berets — would be the best opportunity to actually fight the enemy and make some sort of difference in the war. Zorn said they never knew who they were supposed to be fighting before that. There weren't any real battles or anything. Just sniper attacks and ambushes in the jungle when they were on patrol. Not being sure a lot of the time if someone, one of the Vietnamese people, was a friend or an enemy.

"With the Special Forces I do know he was in the north, near the border. I suspect he went over into Laos, even though they weren't supposed to. He and his team, they worked with Montagnard scouts and organized local people to provide them with intelligence information on the enemy's troop movements. He got to be really close with one of the Montagnards, he told me. Stayed with the man's family and got to know them, too. He said he worried about the Montagnards because they were caught between the North and the South, and really they just wanted everybody to leave them alone."

Greg asked her what a "Montagnard" was. Julie had turned on the speaker phone so we no longer had to crowd so close to hear.

"Like Native Americans here in America," Mrs. Miller said. "The Montagnards lived in the hills and jungles and apparently didn't like the North Vietnamese, so they worked for us. Or we paid them to work for us against the NVA. Sometimes we paid them to go into Laos and do things where our soldiers weren't allowed to go. Officially, I mean.

"Zorn and his friend Fish, after a while they preferred spending their time with the Montagnard people, and their one friend in particular, than they did back at the Special Forces camp. But mostly they were out on patrol, sneaking around the jungle to find out what was happening with the

NVA. Not that he ever told me anything specific about what happened on those patrols. Just that it was like playing Boy Scouts was how he put it. Of course, I know he was just trying to keep me from worrying too much. I know he was probably in the worst place for the war. And I know they had to do some things — their Special Forces units — that regular army or marines couldn't do because they weren't trained for it, and because it took a special kind of person to take on those missions. Zorn never talked about those, either. I've read a lot about it since then, though. Until I just couldn't anymore. It's hard when you know too much."

"Are you okay, Mrs. Miller?" Julie asked. She had stopped talking for a minute.

"Yes," Mrs. Miller said. "It's just — well, nobody has asked about Zorn in so long, and now here I am missing him all over again and wondering all over again about so many things that he kept from me. That he kept from all of us. I mean, he had to, and I understand that, I just wish I could have told Nugent more about his dad. I wish I could have told Nugent *everything* about his dad."

"We're really sorry, Mrs. Miller," Julie said.

"That's all right," Mrs. Miller reassured her. "Is there anything else I can help with?"

"I have a question," I said, speaking for the first time. "I'm Anderson," I added.

"And your question, Anderson?" she asked.

"Well, I guess two questions," I said. "The first one was how come Z, I mean Sergeant Miller, was on the marine base when he went missing. He was in the Special Forces, so he was in the army and not the marines."

"I guess you all need to do more research," Mrs. Miller said, though still sounding nice about it. "Zorn was at a Special Forces camp about five miles away from Khe Sanh. It was a famous battle in its own right, but everybody just sort of includes it in general when they talk about the Siege of Khe Sanh."

"Was he at Lang Vei?" Julie asked. Greg and I looked at her, surprised. We hadn't heard about any Lang Vei before.

"That's right," Mrs. Miller said. "When Lang Vei was overrun by the North Vietnamese, the ones who survived had to fight their way out and they escaped to the marine base. It was ironic, I suppose, because they had pleaded over the radio for help from the marines, but the marine commander wouldn't send help because he thought there would be an ambush, that the whole attack on Lang Vei, where there were only a few dozen Special Forces, was just to draw the marines outside their base so they could be attacked."

"So Sergeant Miller was one of the survivors at Lang Vei?" Greg asked.

"Yes," Mrs. Miller said. "But they never did know how he went missing from the marine base. That was always the big mystery. And still is." She paused for a minute and then asked what my second question was.

"Oh, right," I said. "It was about his friend Fish. I wondered if you knew who he was."

"Well, I never met him," Mrs. Miller said, "but he was kind enough to write to me after Zorn went missing and they never found out what happened. He told me what a good friend and soldier Zorn had been, and how proud I should be of him, and how honored he was to have gotten to serve with Zorn. Those sorts of things. He even sent money not long after Nugent was born. I tried to send it back, but he insisted. I have to say, it was quite a lot of money, and I wish I had been able to convince him that he didn't have to do that. On the other hand, we really did need the help back then, so it was very much appreciated."

"Just one last question," I said. "Do you know Fish's real name?"

"Well, certainly," Mrs. Miller said. "His name was Troutman. Donnie Troutman. I guess you can see why he had the nickname 'Fish.' "

Julie nearly dropped the phone, but somehow held on. "Thank you, Mrs. Miller. We really appreciate your talking with us," she managed to blurt out. "We'll send you a copy of our school paper. Bye!"

I was just staring at Greg. My jaw actually dropped and my mouth fell wide open, though there was no way I could even think about speaking or what I might say.

Greg just stood there like he was frozen. Donnie Troutman was his dad's name, and how many Donnie Troutmans could there be in the world who had served in Vietnam and been in Special Forces?

"Greg?" I finally said after Julie got off the phone. It was the only word that would come out of my mouth. "Greg?"

But he was so much in shock that it didn't seem as if he could even hear me. There was something strange about his eyes, too, which I couldn't figure out until finally it hit me. I'd seen that look before, on Z, and it was the thousand-yard stare. Greg was so lost in whatever he was thinking or feeling that Julie and I could have been anybody and he could have been anywhere.

Julie and I just stood there next to Greg for quite a while, waiting for him to come out of his shock or his trance or whatever.

Finally, after what seemed like a whole hour of us just standing there, Julie touched Greg's shoulder and said his name.

"Are you there?" she asked, her voice not much louder than a whisper.

Greg nodded as if we'd been talking to him all along. "Yeah," he said. "I'm here."

"Wow," I said. "Your dad . . ."

And right then Greg did something I'd never seen him or anybody else do before. He fainted.

·　　·　　·

Julie and I pretty much freaked out, both of us yelling his name and stuff, as if we could call him back into being awake or conscious or whatever. Julie even pulled off his beanie and began using it to fan his face.

Maybe it worked, because when he opened his eyes again he said, "What? What? Why are you yelling at me?"

"Because you fainted!" Julie said, still yelling.

Greg blinked at us a couple of times. He was lying on the floor and we were looking down at him. Then he said,

"Well, would you stop it already? You're giving me a headache."

I thought Julie was going to hit him. Instead, she tossed his beanie at him.

Greg struggled to sit up and I helped him. Julie just crossed her arms and looked annoyed.

"You really did faint," I said. "For a couple of seconds."

Greg shook his head as if trying to get some fog out and stuffed his beanie back on. He got that weird look on his face again, the one he'd had before, or close to it — not exactly the thousand-yard stare, but maybe the hundred-yard stare — and said, "Z knew my dad. They were together in Vietnam."

In all the craziness, I'd nearly forgotten about Z. I looked around now but could see no trace of him, and realized it had been a while since I was sure he was still there with us. I hoped he'd heard everything about Lang Vei, and his Montagnard friend, and especially — most especially — about Greg's dad.

Uncle Dex came over to dinner

at our house that night, so I didn't even get a chance to crash in my room and think over everything that had happened that day.

We had barely started eating when I brought up Vietnam. "So, Uncle Dex," I said, since I just always thought he was the one who knew the most about wars and history and stuff. "That Battle of Khe Sanh, or Siege of Khe Sanh. I mean, I know it was a big battle and all, and the marine base was surrounded, and it went on for like three months or something —"

"Seventy-seven days," Uncle Dex interrupted.

"Yeah, right, that," I said. "I keep reading about how it was such an important battle, too. All battles are important, of course. And it's terrible for anybody to get killed. But what made that one so particularly important, anyway?"

Mom plopped some mashed potatoes down on my plate, and Dad served everybody some kind of chicken casserole he'd made.

"Not exactly what I thought we'd be talking about around the dinner table," Mom said, "but go ahead, Dex."

Dad just laughed.

"From what I always read," Uncle Dex said, "Khe Sanh was a military victory for the U.S., but a public relations nightmare. The numbers they officially released were around two hundred marines and maybe as many as ten to fifteen thousand North Vietnamese KIA. But it was most likely a lot more of us and a lot fewer of them. Casualty figures had a way of being not exactly the most accurate during the war."

"KIA?" I asked, though I could sort of figure it out.

Mom was the one who answered. "It means 'killed in action,'" she said.

Dad, Uncle Dex, and I all stopped eating and just looked at her.

"What?" she said to me. "Do you think you and Uncle Dex were the only ones in the family who inherited Pop Pop's love of history and studying about wars?"

Mom laid her fork across her plate. "The North Vietnamese, even though they kept losing so many of their men to the terrible daily aerial bombing, were hoping to draw the marines off the base and attack them when they were vulnerable," she said.

"Right," Uncle Dex said. "And the longer they had the marines on the defensive, and surrounded, the worse it looked in the TV news reports. We were losing men of our own, a lot of men, and here we were supposed to be winning this war, which was becoming more and more unpopular back home, and every night on the six o'clock news there were war correspondents reporting on the latest from this never-ending siege at Khe Sanh.

"People were growing tired of the war."

"And then there was the Tet Offensive," Mom said. "Don't forget about that."

"Right," Uncle Dex said.

"You said something about that yesterday," I said to Uncle Dex. "But I still don't know what it is."

"Shortly after the NVA attacked Khe Sanh," Mom said, answering for Uncle Dex, who had a mouthful of potatoes, "there were coordinated attacks on cities and military bases all across South Vietnam, mainly by the guerilla fighters, the Viet Cong. Eighty thousand of them. They even overran the U.S. embassy in Saigon, which was the capital of South Vietnam. A lot of people thought that the attack on Khe Sanh was meant to be a diversion so the North Vietnamese and the Viet Cong could successfully mount the Tet Offensive."

"Tet is the Vietnamese new year," Uncle Dex interjected after he swallowed his food. "Everybody was supposed to be dancing and partying and celebrating, and instead the South Vietnamese Army and all the U.S. military were dropping everything to fight off the Viet Cong and NVA."

"What happened?" I asked, worried, as if it was still going on.

"Many people were killed," Mom said, "and there was massive destruction, especially in some of the cities in the north, but in the end it was another military disaster for the North Vietnamese."

"Yeah," Uncle Dex said, "but once again it was a public relations disaster for us and for the South Vietnamese. We'd been fighting this war for so many years already —"

"And the French had been fighting it before us," Mom added. "For ten years."

Uncle Dex picked up where he'd left off. "And here was one more thing, when the president, Lyndon Johnson, kept telling us we were winning, here all of a sudden there are our enemies taking over the embassy, even if it was just for a couple of days. So both things — the Siege of Khe Sanh and the Tet Offensive — turned more and more people back here in America against the war. President Johnson was embarrassed. And there were more of our men coming home in body bags. It was a terrible time."

Dad hadn't said much of anything throughout the conversation. Until now. "Before the U.S. got involved, France had ruled Vietnam for a couple of hundred years as one of their colonies," he said. "The people in the North fought a war for their independence from France, and in 1954 they finally succeeded, after a battle at a place called Dien Bien Phu. The guerilla army of the North Vietnamese surrounded a French base there and kept it under siege until the French surrendered — and gave North Vietnam their independence. So, now, here the U.S. Marines were, surrounded and under siege at Khe Sanh, and in the newspapers and on TV it was Dien Bien Phu all over again."

My brain was about to explode from all the information —
I couldn't wait to get to my room to write it all down, or
all I could remember, from what Dad and Mom and Uncle
Dex had said, and from Mrs. Miller, and from the books in
the library. I rubbed my temples really hard, to see if I could
get rid of a low-grade headache but also to make sure everything I'd learned in the past few days stayed in.

Everybody had settled back into quietly eating for a minute. I really wished I could tell them about Z, and I especially
wished I could tell them about Greg's dad and how he was
Z's friend in the Special Forces.

I wondered what was going on at their house — if Greg
had been able to bring everything up. And I wondered if Z
was sitting in my room right now, waiting for me so we could
talk about the phone call from his wife, and about the things
she said, and about Fish.

"What's the matter, Anderson?" Mom asked. "You look
like you went away for a while there."

They were all looking at me. "I just wish Vietnam had
been like World War II," I said.

"That's a strange thing to say," Dad said. "What do
you mean?"

I fiddled with my fork on my plate for a second, collecting my thoughts. "Well, it's just that in World War II everybody knew why we had to fight that war, and who the good guys were and who the bad guys were. The Germans and the Japanese did all these horrible things, and we went to war to protect the rest of Europe, and all those other countries in Asia, and ourselves."

Uncle Dex chimed in. "But Vietnam was different," he offered.

"Yeah," I said. "We didn't know who the enemy was a lot of the time. And it wasn't like we were always the good guys, exactly. And we didn't even win."

Mom nodded. "That's all true," she said. "But you have to remember, Anderson. Soldiers don't make the decision to go to war. They don't decide what wars we're going to fight. The people we elect to office make those decisions, and we hope and trust that they make the right decisions, but sometimes they don't. But that doesn't mean our soldiers are any less brave, and it doesn't mean that their sacrifices have any less meaning, because they're doing it for us, and they deserve our respect and our support and our appreciation for that. Always."

For some reason I felt like I might cry when Mom said all that. My lip even started trembling a little bit. I really wished I could magically fix things for Z, and for Greg's dad, and for all the veterans who might be out there having a hard time finding their peace or whatever, whether they were living or whether they were dead.

CHAPTER 20

After dinner I went to my room, hoping Z would be there again, but he wasn't. I tried calling Greg, but he didn't answer, so then I called Julie.

She didn't even say hi, she just started talking. "I already found out a lot more about Lang Vei," she said. "Want me to come over and fill you in?"

I was tired all the way down to my bones, but felt like we didn't have time to rest until we had all the answers, so I said yes, that would be great.

I texted Greg while I waited for Julie — *What about ur dad? Did u talk 2 him yet? J is on her way over. Want 2 come 2?* — but didn't hear back from my text, either. I was about

to send him another one — just a bunch of question marks —
but Julie was there before I had time.

"I told my parents we had to study," she said. "Test on
Monday."

I was just about to reply when somebody else interrupted.
It was Z, making a sort of grunting sound like he didn't
approve of something. I hadn't heard him show up, but that
wasn't exactly unusual.

"You shouldn't tell stories to your mom and dad," he said
from his usual place on the floor, leaning against the wall.
"It's not a nice thing to do, and you always get in trouble."

Julie blushed with embarrassment.

"We don't usually," I said. "Except it's hard to be running around helping out ghosts and all. I mean, you have to
tell your parents *something*."

"I guess," Z said. "But keep the storytelling to a
minimum."

"Yes, sir," I said.

He raised one eyebrow.

"I mean, yes, Sergeant," I quickly corrected myself.

Julie changed the subject. "Did you hear any of the conversation with your wife — with Mrs. Miller? She told us a
lot of things. She told us about Lang Vei," she said.

"I did hear most of it," Z said. "From where I was I kind of had to strain to catch everything. When I'm not all there it's like being stuck in a closet and pressing my ear to the door trying to eavesdrop. But it sure was sweet to hear her voice, even from so far away."

He smiled.

"Did you remember how they overran your camp?" Julie asked. "I read about that. The North Vietnamese. And did you remember how you all radioed the marines to help you but they wouldn't come? And how you lost half of your men — half of your Special Forces men — and you and the others barely escaped, and you fought your way to Khe Sanh, to the marine base, even though they wouldn't send help?"

"Slow down, now," Z said. "Just slow down a second. Take a deep breath."

Julie and I both did, even though she was the only one talking. "I just got excited," Julie said.

"And I appreciate that," Z said. "Just don't want you to start hyperventilating or anything. Plus, I've been remembering some things, too."

"Like what?" I asked, eager to hear.

Z paused for a second. "Shouldn't we wait for your buddy Greg? I'd be mighty interested to hear about how things went with him and Fish. That must have been quite a shock for him to realize who his dad was all along. Sure was a shock to me."

"He fainted," I said. "But he's okay. At least, he's okay from the fainting."

"We caught him," Julie interjected. "Before he fell."

"I kind of had a sense of that," Z said. "Even though I wasn't there enough to exactly see it. Anyway, I tried to follow him to his house, hoping I could get to see Fish again after all these years, but I lost the way. Fog got too thick, you might say."

I looked at Julie and she looked at me. It wasn't foggy out at all. But I guess that wasn't the kind of fog he was talking about.

"I called him and texted him," I said. "No answer, though."

Z looked perplexed. "What's that mean — you texted him? What's 'texted'?"

Julie explained. "With our phones, we can type a message instead of dialing and speaking to the person. That's called texting."

"Oh," Z said. "Never heard of that before. But anyway, Fish was a good guy. I know he must be a good dad, too.

Hard to talk about the war, though, unless it's with some-body else who's been there. I hope Greg isn't expecting too much if he brings it up with his dad. Not right away. Maybe if Fish has time to warm up to it and all. I always had a hard time trying to talk about it, even with Philomena."

"Greg wasn't sure if he would talk about it," I said. "Mr. Troutman has kind of a hard time and Greg's mom told him it was because of the war. Sometimes his dad drinks and Greg doesn't like to be around when that happens so he comes over here."

I wasn't sure why I was telling Z all that, but from the way he was nodding it seemed like the right thing to do.

"I can understand," he said. "Wish it wasn't so, but I get it."

Z started flickering. Julie noticed it first. "You're disap-pearing again," she said. "Can you tell us about Lang Vei before you go this time? Anything that I might not have read?"

"Yeah," I chimed in. "And we can try to show you the way to Greg's. We might be able to help. It's not far from here. Just a couple of blocks. We can take you over to see Mr. Troutman, I mean, Fish."

Z's voice was breaking up, but he tried the best he could, even with the growing static. "Wasn't just us, Special Forces," he said. "Was Montagnards. Had nine hundred in the camp. Families, too. They were on our side. NVA wanted them as dead as they wanted us dead. Couldn't abandon them. Had to stay and fight until couldn't anymore. Not right to leave them behind. Hundreds of them went down. Rest fled when we did. Took to the countryside. NVA had tanks. Tanks! Nobody'd ever seen that before. Not from the North. Couldn't stop them. Tried the best we could. Way outnumbered. Fighting too close to call in air support. No reinforcements. Marines five miles away but wouldn't come. Not that I blamed them. Was all a big trap. Everybody knew it."

If he said anything else we couldn't hear it any more than we could see him now. Once again he was gone, voice and all.

· · ·

Julie and I sat there quietly for a minute, and then both of us slumped — me onto the bed and her in the chair at my desk.

"I'm tired," I said.

"Me too," Julie said, which surprised me. I didn't think Julie ever got tired. I wasn't totally sure that she even slept at night, judging from all the reading and research and stuff she was always doing.

"Should we take a break from all this?" I asked.

Julie sat up. "I don't think we can," she said. "You saw how he faded out just now. He seems frail to me. He's having a harder and harder time holding together and being with us. I think we don't have much time left."

"But it hasn't been that long," I said. "Our first ghost took weeks before he started fading out. Remember William Foxwell?"

"Yeah," Julie said. "I think it is different with every ghost, the same way that every person is different. Some ghosts, perhaps they have more control about how long they can be around, and about where they can go. Others, maybe they can only be close to us — to the Kitchen Sink or to your room or to all three of us — or two of us — when we're together. I think Z doesn't have very much control over when he can be around. And it must also be different — how much time each ghost has once they show up."

"You mean, how much time for us to help them solve their mysteries before it's too late to help them?" I asked.

Julie nodded sadly.

We both just sat there for a while, letting everything sink in. It all made sense, what Julie had just said. Not that I liked hearing it, or thinking about it. I just wanted to solve the mystery and help Z and have everybody live happily ever after. Or maybe not *live*, but, you know, whatever.

After a while, I asked Julie if there was anything else about Lang Vei that she'd found out that might help us — and him.

"Mostly just what Z said," Julie replied. "It was a small camp for the Green Berets. They did secret missions and surveillance missions. They recruited the Montagnard people to help fight the North Vietnamese, and to travel across the border into Laos for surveillance and to ambush the NVA supply lines on the Ho Chi Minh Trail. Things like that. What Mrs. Miller had already told us, too. Some of the Montagnard people were part of the Green Beret teams, like their scouts and their translators. They hated the North Vietnamese Army."

"Anything else?" I asked.

"Only that it was a terrible battle at the Special Forces camp, and as Sergeant Miller said, they were outnumbered ten to one, or more, and the NVA had tanks. Many, many Special Forces and Montagnard people were killed. Sergeant Miller and Greg's father — they were among the few who escaped.

"And meanwhile at Khe Sanh — the NVA kept bombing the base, and trying to penetrate it with their ground soldiers. And they endured so much bombing by the U.S., day after day after day. There were hidden sensors all through the jungle to detect the NVA movements, and that's one way we knew where to drop bombs on them from our planes."

I shook my head, just thinking about how awful all of it must have been — not just for our guys, but for the NVA troops, too. Probably even worse for them.

"One more thing," Julie said. "Sergeant Miller didn't mention this, and maybe he didn't remember it yet."

"What?" I asked.

"The Montagnard people he talked about — who were in the Special Forces camp at Lang Vei and fought with the Green Berets — many of them who escaped, and many more in villages in that area, they also went to the marine base at Khe Sanh for protection." Julie was more animated than usual as she was telling me this, poised on the edge of her chair as if she might jump up at any second.

"They were afraid of the North Vietnamese, that they would be killed, and their families would be killed now that the NVA were all over the area and controlling the countryside," Julie continued. "But when they went to the marine base, first the marines took all their weapons, and then the marines turned them away."

I was the one who jumped up. "Why? They were like our allies! They were fighting on our side!"

"I know," Julie said. "But the marines thought it might be another trick. That some of the Montagnard people might be on the side of the NVA, and might help the NVA attack the base once they were inside. So they refused to let the Montagnard people in."

"What happened to them?" I asked, still worked up. Z had just been telling us how loyal the Montagnards were to the Special Forces.

Julie shook her head. "I think many of them had to leave their homes forever. And I think many of them were killed by the North Vietnamese."

CHAPTER 21

Julie and I were sitting together at lunch the next day, both of us still tired, neither of us saying much, picking over our lunches, when a shadow darkened the table. I knew without even looking up that it was Belman.

"Where's the third little musketeer?" he asked, laughing. His friends laughed dutifully along, right on cue.

I still didn't look up. Julie didn't, either. She just said, "He's peeing in your locker."

I nearly died.

Belman freaked out. "He's what? I'll kill that twerp!"

"Just kidding," Julie said, showing a sudden interest in her lunch.

"Not funny, Julie," Belman snarled. This surprised me, too. He knew Julie's name?

Julie must have had the same reaction. "You know my name?" she asked.

"Lucky guess," Belman said. "Quick question: Is the Bomb Squad playing at the All-Ages Open Mic Night on Saturday? Inquiring minds want to know."

"We're not the Bomb Squad," I corrected him, though it occurred to me that when you said it and thought about it in the right way, that might not be a bad name for a band. "And anyway, what do you care?"

"Ignore him," Julie said to me, obviously too late.

"Just wondering," Belman said, already laughing at the next joke he was planning to tell at our expense. "Wondering if we should wear hazmat suits, that is!"

His friends made sure he knew that they thought he was the funniest guy on the planet. I thought Julie was going to stab him with a fork, but she somehow managed to stay calm until they left.

"One of these days . . . ," she said, though she didn't finish the thought. She didn't have to.

．　　．　　．

I saw Greg in class that afternoon and tried to talk to him afterward, but he sort of waved me off. "Sorry, Anderson," he said. "I just kind of need some time to think about stuff."

"It's okay," I said. "I mean, I was worried that you didn't answer my phone calls or my texts or anything."

Greg just shrugged. "I didn't really want to talk to any-body," he said. "Maybe later."

And just like that he walked off down the hall.

I didn't see him again the rest of the day, or that night, or the next day at school, either. I sent him more texts and left some more voice mails, but nothing. I was starting to feel like a total stalker or something, but I was worried about him. Nobody even answered when I called his house phone on Tuesday. Not even his dad.

Z hadn't shown up again, either — not Sunday night after Julie went home and not Monday night, even though I stayed up until way past midnight hoping I'd hear something from Greg, and not Tuesday morning when Mom dragged me out of bed to eat breakfast and send me stumbling off to school. I felt like a zombie from lack of sleep and from being stressed-out about helping Z, and now worrying about Greg on top of everything else. Worrying about him a lot.

Julie must have been reading my mind when we met up at lunch because she nudged my shoulder with her elbow. "He'll be okay," she said. "I know he'll be okay."

"Yeah?" I asked. "Then why hasn't he been in touch? Greg is always calling me and texting me and coming over to stay at my house, even when we aren't trying to save ghosts."

"This is different," Julie said, sounding kind of wise for a sixth grader. "It's about what is between him and his dad. They just need some time, I think."

·   ·   ·

Julie and I went by Greg's house that afternoon after school, but nobody answered the door and his dad's truck wasn't there.

"His dad could just be at work," Julie said.

"But what about Greg?" I asked.

"Knock louder," Julie said.

I looked at my red knuckles. "I already did," I said.

"Text him again," she suggested.

"I think ten times is enough," I said, not used to being the reasonable one in a conversation with Julie.

"You're right," Julie said. "Why don't we just go to Uncle Dex's and practice for the all-ages thing."

I just stood there for a minute and blinked at her. "How can you think about that when Greg is missing?"

"He's not missing," she said. "He's just somewhere else. You said it yourself."

I knew this bickering about Greg between Julie and me was just because we were both so worried. Maybe a little band practice would do us some good, or at least take our minds off of everything for a little while.

Fifteen minutes later we were in the basement with our instruments, strumming and plunking our way through Julie's hamster song and then her other song about bullies. I guess my voice sounded okay — she didn't scowl or wince or cringe or anything — but it didn't feel right without Greg there on his guitar.

Uncle Dex came downstairs after a while to check in on us. "Everything all right with you guys?" he asked, taking off his baseball cap and rubbing his head. His hair already looked kind of crazy and was now even crazier until he pulled the cap back on and tamped it down.

"Yeah," I said. "I guess."

"Where's Greg?" he asked, as if that wasn't totally on our minds, anyway.

Julie explained that we didn't know and we hadn't heard from him.

"Hmmm," Uncle Dex said, looking at me. "You two are supposed to be, like, conjoined twins or something, aren't you?"

I shrugged.

"Well, mind if I sit in for a couple of tunes?" Uncle Dex asked. I knew he'd been dying to pull out his ukulele and join us for some time. I was busy trying to think of a good excuse to send him back upstairs when Julie spoke up again.

"Sure," she said, startling me. "We'd love to have you."

"Great!" Uncle Dex said. "I'll just shoot upstairs and get my instrument. Be right back."

As soon as he left I turned to Julie. "Really?" I asked. "*Really?* You want my uncle to play his ukulele with us?"

Julie smiled. "We need something, or somebody, to take our minds off Greg, so why not him?"

Uncle Dex was back with his ukulele before I could even think of an answer.

"So what are we playing?" he asked, and the next thing I knew we were running through our playlist again, this time with the ukulele sort of lightening things up.

"Too bad you're not our age, Uncle Dex," Julie said when we finished, even though Uncle Dex wasn't her uncle, of course.

He laughed. "Well, you're welcome to borrow my ukulele any time you want for your band," he said.

We heard footsteps coming down the stairs just then, and I knew right away it must be Greg. People you've known forever, you can recognize them just from the sounds they make.

"Hi, guys," Greg said, stepping into the practice room. "Did I miss anything?"

Julie flew at Greg and gave him a giant hug. I'm not sure who was surprised more, me or Greg. He just stood there with his mouth gaping open while Julie squeezed him. I'm sure the look on my face was the same.

Julie released Greg and stepped back. "Where have you been?" she asked.

Greg caught my eye and I just shrugged. "We missed you," I said.

You'd have thought Greg had been gone for a year or something, the way we were carrying on. Even Uncle Dex got into the act, offering Greg his ukulele to practice on when he saw Greg hadn't brought his guitar.

Greg held the ukulele up in front of him and studied it for a minute, and then shrugged and said thanks. "I'll give it a try," he said in a soft voice.

I realized he hadn't exactly answered Julie's question and wondered when he'd tell us — and *what* he'd tell us.

Uncle Dex, meanwhile, said he had to get back to work. "Busiest part of the day at a junk shop," he said. "Better head upstairs."

He left, and Julie and I turned to Greg expectantly, now that we had him all to ourselves.

CHAPTER 22

"Well?" Julie asked.

"I guess you want to know where I've been and all." Greg said, hugging the ukulele to his chest and running his fingers over the strings. He plunked out a couple of chords and then stopped.

"Only if you want to tell us," I said, not wanting to sound like he *had* to tell us.

"Of course," Julie said, though I knew she wanted to interrogate him.

Greg played a few more chords, already figuring out the fingering, even though I'd never seen him play a ukulele before. I guess all that guitar practice he'd been doing was paying off in all sorts of ways.

"I thought about it and thought about it and thought about it, and finally I talked to my dad," he said, speaking softly. "I asked him about Z — Sergeant Miller. I kind of had to make up a story about us having a unit on Vietnam in school, and that's why we went to The Wall. And I said maybe my mom must have mentioned Zorn Miller to me, that Dad had had a friend in Vietnam with that name, and we'd seen his name on The Wall."

I thought that sounded like a pretty good cover story, even though I hated that he had to tell a lie to his dad, or that any of us were having to do that to our parents or anybody.

"And then what?" Julie prompted him.

Greg strummed what actually sounded like a song.

"He got really quiet," Greg answered. "And he didn't say anything at first. Not for a long time. I almost thought maybe he didn't hear me, or he was going deaf or something. I mean, we were right there in the living room. It was yesterday afternoon after I got home from school and he got home from work. And then, after a while, he just got up and walked outside. He was raking leaves."

"What did you do?" I asked.

Greg shrugged. "Went outside and raked leaves with him. We did the whole backyard. And it's a big backyard, too. With a lot of trees."

"Then what?" Julie asked.

Greg kind of smiled, though his face still looked strained. "Then we raked the front yard. And bagged up all the leaves. And dragged them around to the curb so they could get picked up."

"So your dad never said anything back?" It was my turn to ask.

"It was weird," Greg said. "I thought he was going to get mad or something, but he didn't. Just quiet, like I said. And we didn't talk the whole time we were working in the yard, either, but it was nice. My dad and me, we don't do too much stuff together, but that was something we did together, even though it was a lot of work."

"I hope he paid you," I said.

Greg rolled his eyes. "It's not about money, Anderson," he said. I apologized.

"Anyway," he continued, "when we finally finished, we went back inside and he had a beer and I had a soda. I was worried that he was going to start, you know, really drinking again, the way he does sometimes. He finished his beer and went back to the refrigerator and stood there for a long time, staring at the other beers, so I was really nervous about it then. But he didn't get one out. He just finally shut the door and told me to come on."

"Come on where?" Julie asked. We were sort of a tag team with the questions.

"I didn't know," Greg said. "Not at first. He asked me something about The Wall and I told him where we went with Uncle Dex, and how they had the directory, and the statues of the soldiers and the nurses. But mostly about The Wall and the things people left there for the people whose names were there, like Zorn Miller. So Dad went into his bedroom and was in there for a bit, and then he came out with something in a bag and he said, 'Come on, Greg,' again, and so I followed him out to the car and we drove back up to Washington."

"Twice in one week?" I said.

"Yep." Greg nodded. "And the other funny thing is Dad seemed kind of, like, cheerful the whole way up, even when we got stuck in traffic for a while. He was just talking about stuff — about work and about things he did when he was a kid. Stuff about his cousins and some kind of farm his aunt and uncle had, and how they used to climb up on hay bales and swing on ropes in the barn and milk sheep or something."

"You don't milk sheep," Julie said.

"I know," said Greg. "Anyway, before you know it we were there, back at The Wall. Me and my dad."

"That must have been so strange," I said.

"Yeah," Greg said. "But he didn't even hesitate, just marched right over there from where we parked the truck. I almost had to run to keep up with him. Once we got there, though, right at the tip of The Wall, he stopped and just stared at it for a while."

"Did he say anything?" Julie asked.

Greg nodded, his hands still holding on to that ukulele like it was protecting him from something. "He said, 'All those names.'"

"That was all?" Julie asked.

"Pretty much," Greg said. "At first, anyway. Then, after we stood there for a really long time, he asked me to show him where he could see Z's name, so I did. I even held his hand and led him there, which I guess was the weirdest part. I mean, I haven't held hands with my dad in I don't know how long. And I'm pretty sure he hasn't hugged me in forever, either. He's just not a huggy guy, you know? But when we got there and I pointed to Z's name, Dad looked at it for what seemed like ten minutes, and I looked at Dad's reflection, which I guess he was sort of looking at, too, even though it was nighttime. But since you can go there twenty-four hours a day, it's lit up so you can still see. And the whole time he had his eyes on Z's name. And then he sat down right there on the walkway in front of Z's panel and he pulled out three things from the bag he was carrying."

"Which were what?" I asked.

"One was a picture of the two of them just standing there with their arms over each other's shoulders and giving the peace sign, which is pretty funny since they both have guns and bandoliers and helmets and war stuff on. The second thing was a letter that had Z's name on it, which Dad must have written to Z when he was in the bedroom earlier getting the stuff that was in the bag he brought. He didn't show it to me or tell me what it said, and I didn't ask him, either, since I could just tell it was meant to be private. And then the third thing was my dad's medals. And that's when Dad said the only thing he said the whole time we were sitting there."

Greg paused for a second and then continued. "He said, 'Z deserved these a lot more than me.' And then he laid the medals on top of the letter and the photo there at the base of The Wall under Z's panel. And then Dad put his arm around me and hugged me and we sat there like that for about another hour. I think my dad might have been praying or something, and I said a prayer, too."

Greg turned his attention back to the ukulele and started strumming it again, this time humming to himself, a tune that sounded vaguely familiar, like I'd heard it before but I couldn't place it and it didn't sound like anything we'd been playing in our band.

Julie and I looked at each other, and shrugged, and turned back to him.

"Did you ask him about, you know, what happened to Z?" I asked.

"Yes," Julie echoed. "What happened to him? How he went missing in action? Did your dad know anything about that?"

Greg looked up. "Oh yeah," he said. "I mean, he eventually told me. That part was strange, too. I didn't want to push him to talk about anything else after The Wall. Dad just seemed so quiet and kind of emotional and all. He wasn't crying or anything, but, well, it's hard to explain. Anyway, I just thought it was a good idea to just stay quiet myself, you know? And wait to see if he wanted to talk or anything. So it was really, really late when we got home and he hadn't said much the whole way back, even when we stopped to get something to eat. And I hadn't brought my phone with me so I didn't even see that you guys had left all those messages and stuff until this afternoon, because I was so tired and went straight to bed once we got back.

"And then, like, an hour later, Dad came in and sat on my bed and he just started talking — about Z, and about what happened to him in Vietnam."

"Oh wow," I said. "I sure wish Z would show up right now to hear all this."

"Yeah, but that's the crazy thing about it," Greg said.

"What?" asked Julie. "What was the crazy thing?"

"That when my dad came into the bedroom to talk to me, Z was there, too. I mean, I couldn't see him, and of course my dad totally couldn't see him, but I just somehow kind of knew he was there the whole time."

"But how?" I asked.

Julie had the answer. "Don't you remember, Anderson? You told Z where Greg lived. Sort of. You said it was just a couple of blocks from here. And he tried to follow Greg, but got lost in the fog. He must have found his way there."

Greg just said, "I guess so, or whatever. I just know he was there, and what my dad told me — told *us* — it was pretty much the end of the mystery."

CHAPTER 23

"So Dad told me all about what happened at Lang Vei," Greg began. "He got really worked up talking about it, too, even though it's been more than forty years. I kind of had this feeling that Z was getting worked up hearing Dad talk about it, too, even though I couldn't see him or anything. I guess you never get over something like that, whether you survived it like my dad, or whether you're a ghost like Z. Dad said so many of the Montagnards got killed at Lang Vei, hundreds of them. He said we owed the rest of them so much, because they'd fought alongside the Green Berets, and they'd fought for our side for years, and their families were at risk from the NVA in their villages."

I interrupted. "But the marines thought letting the Montagnards into the base could be a trick," I said. "That's what Z told us and what Julie read. There could have been spies or traitors or whatever in with the Montagnards who showed up at Khe Sanh."

Greg kept nodding. "Yeah, Dad told me that, too. And he said on the one hand he understood all that, but on the other hand, in just a couple of days there were, like, thousands of Montagnards begging to be let into the base for protection, because they knew if they stayed in their villages they might be slaughtered or put in prison camps or whatever. But the marines turned them away anyway."

Greg stopped talking for a minute and fiddled with the ukulele. Not really playing it, more just running his hands over the wood and strings.

Then he took up where he'd left off. "There was this one Montagnard guy, they just called him by his first name, Nay, who had worked with their Special Forces team as a scout and guide. My dad and Z spent a lot of time with Nay and even lived with Nay's family in their village off and on over, like, a year.

"So when Nay came to the marine base with his family a week after the attack on Lang Vei, Dad and Z argued with the marines that they had to at least let them in — that the NVA would kill all of Nay's family if they didn't. But the marine guards said orders were orders, even though Dad could tell they were sympathetic. Nobody liked turning the Montagnards away, but at the same time they knew what could happen if even just one of them turned out to be a spy, or even somebody who could sabotage the ammunition dump again on the base, or the air field or whatever. So they ordered Nay to give up his M16 that he'd gotten from the Special Forces, and all his other weapons. And then they sent him and his family away, along with everybody else."

Julie was outraged all over again. "I can't believe they did that! It wasn't right!"

Greg shrugged. "It was complicated," he said. "I guess as hard as it was, my dad sort of understood it, but Z just couldn't get over it. Dad said Z stayed up all that night just furious at what he saw as this enormous betrayal of the Montagnards, and especially of Nay and his family. I mean, Nay had risked his life for Dad and Z on a bunch of occasions. My dad said Nay had probably saved their lives a bunch of times, too.

"So finally, at about, like, three o'clock in the morning — Dad remembered it was Valentine's Day of all things — Z told my dad he was going outside the wire to find Nay and help his family somehow, help them escape from the Central Highlands to somewhere that they'd be safe from the NVA."

"Outside the wire?" Julie asked.

I knew that one. "It means he was going to leave the base, go through the wires and stuff that they had all around the base for protection."

Greg just said "Yeah." Then he continued, "Dad argued with Z, told him that would be desertion and he could get court-martialed and even go to military prison. He would get a dishonorable discharge. And he would probably get killed himself. But Z wouldn't listen to Dad. He just said he didn't have a choice, that he had to go. That he owed it to Nay and to the Montagnards. He said that already the Montagnards were suffering from being in the middle of the fight between North and South Vietnam, and he just couldn't sit by and let something terrible happen to Nay.

"And then he left."

"But how?" I asked. "There were marine guards everywhere, all that wire, and land mines and booby traps, not to mention the NVA who had them all trapped on the base."

Greg nodded. "I asked Dad that and he actually smiled, and he just said, 'He was a Green Beret, son. That's what we were trained to do.'"

Greg hesitated. "And then he said something else, which just about knocked me out."

"What?" Julie asked, standing up now and pacing around the room in her nervousness about the story.

Greg swallowed hard. "He said Z turned himself into a ghost and vanished into the night."

.   .   .

It took us a few minutes to pick up the conversation again. A strange sort of breeze blew through the practice room — something that had happened a couple of times with our first ghost — and I wondered, and hoped, that it was Z back with us

And then Greg started talking again.

"Dad was really upset after Z left, but he knew he couldn't tell anybody anything about what Z was doing, or else all the things he'd said to Z — about him being court-martialed and stuff for desertion — would definitely happen. He just kept praying and praying that Z would come back, that he'd show up again, that he'd somehow survive. And Dad felt terribly guilty about the whole thing, too — that he hadn't gone with Z to try to save Nay and his family, that he'd let Z go in the first place. At one point he even told me he should have shot Z — like in the arm or leg or something — to keep him from going.

"But anyway, Dad and the other Special Forces guys, the ones that could still fight, were busy from then on helping defend Khe Sanh for the next two months until all the Air Force bombing of the NVA positions finally broke the siege."

Julie was still pacing. "Surely they searched for Z then?" she asked.

"Yeah," Greg said. "Since Dad hadn't said anything, it was this great mystery how a guy could just disappear from the base, but nobody had an answer. And then afterward, they were busy trying to chase down the NVA units still in the Central Highlands in this big sort of counterattack operation that went on for more months. But Dad made sure he went everywhere he could think of to find Z, and when that never happened he went in search of Nay. To Nay's old village, other villages, even some places over the border in Laos. He said so many of the Montagnards had fled the area by then. And so many others had been killed. But Dad never stopped searching."

"But he found Nay, right?" I asked, or more like demanded. I could hardly stand the suspense of Greg's story, and I was worried sick about how it was going to turn out.

"Yeah," Greg said. "Just one day in Saigon, months later, when Dad was sent down there in the south for something. Like R&R maybe — you know, rest and relaxation — time off from being in combat. However it happened, Nay was so happy to see my dad. He said it was a miracle for his family to have escaped the Central Highlands and for Dad and him to meet again. Nay said that after they were turned away at Khe Sanh by the marines, he and his family hid in a secret cave that Z and my dad and Nay had discovered months earlier, and where they kept supplies and ammunition. Z thought to look for them there, and sure enough, that's where he found them. They had a secret signal, so when Z finally got to the cave he let out this whistle. My dad even did the whistle for me."

Greg demonstrated for us. Three short tweets, two long, and then this sort of trilling sound.

Then he continued with the story. "Nay said he couldn't believe Z had managed to get through the NVA lines to find them, that they had almost given up hope, and were sure they would be captured and all killed, or worse. Z had maps and he laid them out to show Nay the way he needed to go to escape and make his way south with his family. They kept thanking Z over and over, but he said there wasn't any time; that he'd seen NVA patrols, and Nay and his family needed to leave that night. Z gave them all the money he had, and the maps, and led them away from the cave, a couple of miles through the jungle and out of the hills."

Greg wiped his forehead. He was sweating now, I guess from telling the story and getting all worked up about it. I was getting worked up, too.

"Then Z stopped and pointed Nay and his family in the direction they needed to go. Nay asked Z what he would do now, and Z said he had to get back to Khe Sanh. He shook Nay's hand and saluted Nay's two children. He told Nay that he was going to be a father soon, too, and Nay said he already knew that because Z must have told him twenty times already. Z just laughed, and then he left, back up the trail."

Greg was tearing up now, and I suddenly wasn't so sure I wanted to hear what came next. Julie asked him, though, so Greg finished the story.

"There was a land mine," he said, his voice now very quiet. "It was a miracle nobody had stepped on it before, on the way down the trail. But Z wasn't lucky this time. Nay was watching Z as he left. Nay saw what happened when the land mine detonated."

Greg couldn't finish, not right away, but he didn't have to, because now we knew. I looked around the room again, hoping there would be some sign of Z still with us.

Julie asked one more question. "Did he suffer?"

Greg shook his head no.

Nay and his wife dug a shallow grave for Z. The explosion had been terrible. There was very little they could bury. They had to leave quickly before the enemy returned, but they still stayed long enough to pile stones over the freshly turned earth.

"But why didn't your dad ever tell anybody?" I asked Greg. "Did he even tell Z's wife?"

"He was afraid that Z would be charged with desertion," Greg said, "even though he had been killed, and even though everything Z did was to help save Nay and his family. And if there was the desertion charge, Philomena and Nugent would lose their benefits. They'd lose their house. They'd lose everything. Dad didn't even want to risk Philomena knowing, and putting the burden on her. So all these years, he kept it to himself."

CHAPTER 24

We waited and waited all the
rest of that week for Z to come back to us. Or just for some
sign from Z that he was okay, and that he could go on
now to his rest and his peace in the afterlife, or whatever
came next.

But he didn't show up — not at Uncle Dex's store in our
basement practice room, not at school, not at my house or in
my bedroom or anywhere. There was just nothing.

Greg and Julie and I were bummed, even when we con-
vinced ourselves to keep practicing for the next All-Ages
Open Mic Night. Not that any of us were too excited about
it. The only bright spot all that week — bright for Greg,

anyway — was when his dad, who never took him anywhere, said he'd drive us to the Open Mic Night on Saturday.
He even told Greg he thought he'd like to hear us play.

And Greg's dad also told him that he thought they
should take a trip soon out to California — to Barstow. That
maybe it was time, long past time, that he told Mrs. Miller
and Nugent the rest of the story about what happened to Z.

"Can you believe it?" Greg said, incredulous. It was
Friday afternoon. Just one more practice day before the
open mic competition. "This is my dad we're talking about.
My dad!"

"Yeah," I said, happy for Greg that it seemed at least one
good thing had come out of us trying to help Z. "That's
awesome."

I prayed just before crawling into my bed that night —
for things to somehow still work out right for Z, and for
things to keep working out right for Greg and his dad, too.

Mom and Dad both asked me a couple of times what
was going on, and they said I seemed distracted and was
there anything they could do? But of course there wasn't
anything I could say, because you can't explain about ghosts
to people who don't see them, even your parents. Maybe
especially your parents.

Belman bugged us a couple of times that week at school, but we all reacted pretty much the same way: We just ignored him. Nobody had the energy to even get mad or offended.

We found out one more thing about the Siege of Khe Sanh, in the meantime. That after all the bombings and assaults and explosions and death, the Americans finally broke the siege — and then, within just a few months, closed down the base at Khe Sanh, after all. Something we could have done months earlier and saved so many lives, on our side and on theirs.

The war continued for five more years, with support back home getting weaker and weaker until finally we brought all the troops home and left the South Vietnamese to defend their own country. Two years after that, the North conquered the South and reunited all of Vietnam. The war was officially over. Whatever we'd been doing over there, whatever we'd been fighting for and trying to accomplish, I was pretty sure we'd failed.

I got really down when we read all that, until I thought about what Mom had said about the soldiers who fought in the war — how no matter what we thought of the reasons they were sent, we should always remember that they went over because they had a job to do, and that most of them did it as well as they could, serving and sacrificing for the rest of us, and how they deserved our appreciation, and our love, and our respect.

．．．

Saturday night came way too soon for me. I was already nervous about having to be the new lead singer for the Ghosts of War, but I hadn't counted on just *how* nervous.

Unfortunately, I found that out once it was our turn onstage. We got set up okay — Julie with her keyboard, Greg and me with our guitars, plus our amplifiers and microphones and monitors.

Our first tune was that hamster song of Julie's. "You guys ready?" she asked.

"Definitely," Greg said.

I looked out over the fifty kids in the audience. Belman and his friends were standing on one side, already laughing at us. I saw an elementary school kid picking his nose and another one yawning like it was past her bedtime.

"Uh, yeah, sure," I said, although my palms were sweating and I was having trouble holding on to my guitar pick.

Julie nodded and right away started playing this short keyboard intro. I took a deep breath, wiped my hands on my jeans, and then Greg and I came in on our guitars, actually sounding okay, which totally surprised me. Or at least not too bad, compared to the first All-Ages Open Mic Night when we couldn't even tune our instruments right.

So far, so good.

But then when it was time for me to step up to the mic, I froze. I couldn't remember what I was supposed to be singing, and then I forgot what chords I was supposed to be playing.

Julie and Greg looked over at me frantically. This couldn't be happening, only it was. I had stage fright so bad that I couldn't even move. I stopped playing. I opened my mouth to try singing again, but nothing came out except, "Excuse me. I'll be right back."

And then I ran off the stage, out the side door of the concert warehouse, and threw up in the grass.

At first I didn't hear anything, but then I heard everybody back inside erupting with laughter. I knew I could never go back — not to finish the performance, not ever. I was going to have to transfer schools, find new friends, go into the Witness Protection Program. It was the most embarrassing thing that had ever happened to anybody.

And then a funny thing happened. The laughter kind of died down and I heard the faint strains of a ukulele.

And then I heard Greg's wobbly voice on the microphone, singing.

I opened the door and peeked inside, and sure enough, there was Greg with Uncle Dex's ukulele. I hadn't even noticed that he'd brought it with him to the concert.

He was just standing there at the microphone by himself, strumming and singing away, even though his voice kept cracking.

It was one of those old Vietnam War songs that Uncle Dex had sung for us on our trip to The Wall: "The Ballad of the Green Berets."

I stepped inside so I could see and hear better, though I didn't go back onstage right away. At first some kids were still laughing, and then snickering — especially Belman. But the more Greg sang, the less they laughed, and once he got to the chorus, everybody just stood there quietly, listening. I thought Julie would be mad — about me getting stage fright and running away, about Greg singing a song by himself that we hadn't practiced — but she actually had this kind of sweet look on her face as she sat at her keyboard, watching and listening to Greg.

I inched farther in until I was at the edge of the stage,

and then I managed to climb back up, though I stayed behind the amps and stuff.

Greg kept strumming and singing. He had figured out a sort of Hawaiian arrangement, so it sounded pretty different from how Uncle Dex had played it, though still all the same words.

And then I saw, way in the back of the crowd of kids, Greg's dad. He must have heard Greg, too, and come in from the parents' waiting area to check it out. Even from where I was up onstage I could tell he had tears in his eyes.

Julie looked back at me and smiled, and I shrugged and mouthed the word "Sorry" and smiled back. I pointed to Greg's dad and she nodded. She'd seen him, too.

Greg was on the last verse now and I could see a lot of kids' heads nodding in what I took to be appreciation.

And when I looked again at Greg's dad I got yet another shock, because there, standing next to him, was Z. Julie must have seen him, too, because she glanced over at me again and our eyes met and then we both just turned back and stared.

Z and Fish. Just for this one moment, together again, although it must have been the very last of the energy Z had for this sort of thing because he was already starting to fade.

Greg finished and all the kids applauded — even Belman and his friends. Greg's dad and Z lifted their hands and both gave the peace sign, just like in that picture Greg had told us about that his dad left at The Wall.

And then Z was gone, only this time it was forever.

· · ·

We somehow managed to get through our set after that, and I somehow got over my stage fright enough to sing two of our songs. We came in fourth in the competition, which we all decided was pretty good, although there were only five bands. Still a definite improvement over the last time, when we finished dead last.

"No telling what we can do if we get serious about practicing," Julie said as we piled into Greg's dad's truck afterward with all our equipment.

"And if Anderson can keep from throwing up," Greg added, elbowing me in the ribs.

"And if we can take a break from ghosts for a while," I said, just loud enough for them to hear.

They both nodded, but I still had the feeling that we weren't through with the real ghosts of war just yet.

The Battle of Khe Sanh, which took place between January 21 and July 6, 1968, is one of the most important and controversial battles of the Vietnam War, and military historians continue to debate the decision to defend the marine base there. The seventy-seven-day siege may have ended in a military victory for the U.S. and South Vietnam, but most agree that it was a public relations disaster, and a major contributing factor in the rapidly declining support in America for the war.

While the characters and story, both those from present day and history, in *Lost at Khe Sanh* are fictional, the stories of the siege, the attack at Lang Vei, and the treatment of the

Montagnard people are all based on fact. There are a number of excellent accounts of the siege at Khe Sanh and the attack on the Green Beret camp at Lang Vei. Two worth checking out are *Valley of Decision: The Siege of Khe Sanh* by John Prados and Ray W. Stubbe, and *Khe Sanh: Siege in the Clouds: An Oral History* by Eric Hammel.

Stanley Karnow's *Vietnam: A History* is generally recognized as the best history of the war, while Philip Caputo's *A Rumor of War* is one of the best memoirs from the conflict. *The Things They Carried* by Tim O'Brien is a powerful book about the war and well worth reading for a fuller understanding of what it was like for those who served.

To find out more about the Vietnam Veterans Memorial in Washington, DC — The Wall — check out the National Park Service site, www.nps.gov/vive/index.htm, and the site for the Vietnam Veterans Memorial Fund, www.vvmf.org. To learn more about the Montagnard people, a great place to start is with Rebecca Onion's article at www.slate.com, "The Snake-Eaters and the Yards."

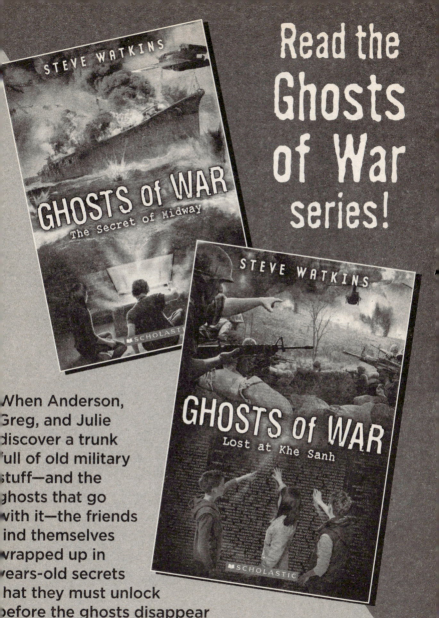

Read the **Ghosts of War** series!

STEVE WATKINS

GHOSTS of WAR
The Secret of Midway

STEVE WATKINS

GHOSTS of WAR
Lost at Khe Sanh

When Anderson, Greg, and Julie discover a trunk full of old military stuff—and the ghosts that go with it—the friends find themselves wrapped up in years-old secrets that they must unlock before the ghosts disappear forever, their mysteries unsolved.

Available in print and eBook editions

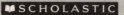

SCHOLASTIC
scholastic.com

GHWAR1